PERSONA

Fishing and Life

*An Obsessive
Weekend Tournament Angler's
Pursuit of Perfection*

A Novel by KURT MAZUREK

1st Edition

Written by Kurt Mazurek
Edited by Joe Shead and Tony Liedl
Cover Design by Kurt Mazurek
Cover Photography by Craig Mazurek

Printed in the United States of America
J.L.S. Mazurek Publishing

First Printing: July 2013

ISBN- 978-1-940474-02-1

Trademark Acknowledgments
The author acknowledges the trademarked status and trademark owners of the following
trademarks mentioned in this work of fiction:
iPhone: Apple, Inc., Bass Pro Shops, Berkley Power Bait: Jarden Corp., Gander Mountain, Ranger Boats:
Fishing Holdings, BASS, FLW Outdoors, Weather Channel, Shimano, Daiwa, Hot Foot, *Bass Wars* by
Nick Taylor, *Knowing Bass* by Keith A. Jones, Ph.D., *Angler's Quest* by Rick Clunn, Gimmie' Three Steps
by Lynyrd Skynyrd, *Ice Cream Man* by Van Halen, *I'm Yours* by Jason Mraz, Senko:Yamamoto, Skeeter
Boats, Ford F-150, Yamaha Marine, Toyota Tundra, Minn Kota, Chug Bug:Storm, Holiday Inn, Triton
Boats, Pop-R: Rebel, Zip-Lock Bags, *The Terminator, Edward Scissor Hands*, Strawberry Quick, *The Little
Mermaid*:Disney, Dr. Seuss, Sweet Beaver:Reaction Innovations, Mountain Dew, Mello Yello, Bill Buckner,
Chicago Cubs, Major League Baseball, Johnny Depp, Scooby-Doo, U.S. Olympic Committee's: *Top Ten
Guiding Principles for Mental Training*, iTunes:Apple, Rick Clunn, *Mental Training for Winning* by Pierre
Provost, Travis Manson, Rapala, Wal-Mart, Facebook, All-Terrain Jigs, Strike King Lures, Captain Jack
Sparrow: *Pirates of the Caribbean*: Disney, Berkley Havoc Pit Boss Craw, James Bond

In memory of my dad, Wally, the first person to take me fishing

Contents

Ch 1
Maybe This Is My Day

My name is William. If you ask me what I'm thinking about right now, my honest answer will almost always include fish and/or ways to catch more fish.

* * *

The alarm is set for two hours before daylight, but it never gets a chance to sound. I take a deep breath and open my eyes, eager to get this day started. There are fellow competitors who opt for the extra sleep, but I like to have my boat in the water early–first, even. It's funny how getting up for work every other morning feels like it's going to kill me. I fumble around on the night-stand for the sticky, God-knows-who's-been-touching-it, motel TV remote and turn on the local Weather Channel. Of course, I've been studying the weather constantly for the last several days on my iPhone, but watching the Weather Channel in the motel is an old habit.

I get dressed by the dim light of an underpowered, flickering bulb, saving my neatly pressed and hung, tournament day shirt for last. Some of the guys will have shirts loaded with logos of their sponsors. Many have logos merely to fool their competitors into thinking they have sponsors. At this time, I really don't have many logos on my shirt–my father's realty business, Maxon Group Realty of Wausau and D-Licious Hand Poured Baits, a mostly defunct company my brother-in-law, Doug has been working on. I'd feel silly wearing a bunch of fake sponsors, but to be honest, I think a lot about the day I have some real sponsors. It's weird how closely sponsorship is tied to one's perceived ability to catch fish, but that's another story.

I unlock the front door and peer out into the foggy darkness. The cool air reminds me to throw a hoodie on over my jersey. Of course the hoodie is branded with a big Shimano logo, but that's alright because they sent it to me for free when I bought three Chronarch reels a couple years back.

I like to back the boat in as close to my room's door as possible so I can keep an eye on it overnight. For this reason, I usually end up staying in little "mom and pop" motels where this is an option. I know there are nicer rooms at the bigger chains, but I sleep better knowing the boat is close by.

The protective cover is dripping with morning dew, and leaves a cold, wet stripe across the front of my hoodie as I lean into it to unfasten the straps. Now comes the first tense moment of the day. I peel the cover back, and with just one hopeful eye, I peer into the back compartment where the big trolling motor batteries are stored. They need to be recharged every night for the following day's activities. I open my other eye and breathe a small sigh of relief as I spot three green lights on the charging unit, indicating a full charge. Sometimes motel power outlets can be flakey. Sometimes a fellow motel guest can accidentally trip on your extension cord. It's usually fine, but red indicator lights mean you're screwed. Green is good.

Next I begin carrying my rods and tackle boxes from the motel room back out to the boat. This may be overkill on my part, but I've heard too many stories of boats being burglarized in motel parking lots. In a case like this, where the boat is right by the door, I don't necessarily bring everything into the room–it depends on the neighborhood. Honestly, I have no way of knowing if the neighborhood is safe, but I make my best guess. As a precaution, I always bring in the six or seven rigs I know I'm likely to use on tournament day, along with an assortment of appropriate tackle. But let's be honest–I know I'm going to throw a wackey-rigged Senko 90 percent of the time today. Hey, I've caught a lot of bass on that lure. I like solid black.

Another quick walk-through in the room and I'm on my way.

A glance in my rearview mirror reveals the first of my competitors emerging from their rooms. I roll through the first intersection, under the flashing yellow traffic lights and click on the radio. My presets don't work in this town and a quick scan almost always lands on classic rock or country.

"Gimmie Three Steps" just isn't getting me fired up right now, so I opt for silence as I head to the ramp.

I sure hope that gas station I saw yesterday is open 24/7. Even though it's chilly now, I'd really like to grab a bag of ice for the day. Not only will it keep my drinks and snacks cold, I can throw some in the livewell to keep the fish more lively. Weighing in dead fish comes with a hefty penalty, so I'm very conscious about my catch's wellbeing.

It's still completely black as I weave my truck and boat through the parking lot headed toward the four-lane boat launch. Random dots of red, green and white light, scattered across the lot and reflecting on the the water, reveal there are just a handful in the 140-boat field that feel the same way I do about an early start. Fine with me. I try desperately to avoid any feelings of anxiety or pressure to start my tournament day, so I avoid the chaos whenever possible.

Slowly but steadily I back my trailer down the concrete ramp until I see the back end of the boat just begin to float free of the carpeted bunks. I love the amber glow of the trailer's submerged taillights, reminding me of the unknown world beneath the water's black surface.

I climb over the bow and find my place in the drivers seat. The still of night is broken as my high-horsepower, two-stroke outboard motor comes to life and the boat slips easily from the trailer under her power. She's only whispering–a reassuring, confident gurgle for now, but soon she'll be screaming at the top of her lungs. She loves to scream. Once the boat is launched, the only thing left to do is wait. Carefully, I maneuver my way past the other boats.

The guy in the white Ranger recognizes me and we exchange nods. I put the boat in neutral, turn the key off and drift up beside him.

"Hey, Billy Boy!" he says.

"It's William," I correct him, but he doesn't seem to notice.

You gonna leave any for me today?" he asks playfully.

"I just hope I can find five for myself. You're on your own," I counter. We've talked several times before but I'm drawing a blank on his name. White Ranger guy is what I have always called him in my mind.

He takes a loud, deliberate, slurping sip from his gas station coffee. "Get much time to practice?" he inquires.

"Got in Wednesday morning, but there was so much wind I was really just wasting time."

He scowls and gulps down a mouthful of coffee while nodding. "Ugh, tell me about it. Crazy wind."

"So have you got much going?" I ask, hoping for some last-minute clues.

"I'll tell ya what," he says, "I'd win this damned thing if it was a damn northern pike derby!" Then he laughs deeply, like it was the first time anyone had ever said anything like that.

I laugh courteously. He really is a nice guy so I don't mind laughing. But I know he's finished pretty well in other tournaments and I'll bet he's on 'em. I remember when Carl...that's his name, Carl! Carl Marquette! I remember he won this tournament about six years ago. Yep, I'll bet he's got something figured out.

He finishes his coffee, rinses the cup over the side of the boat, and tosses the empty into his rod locker. "Welp, I've got a few things I need to tie up yet," he announces, releasing me from our conversation.

"Yep, me too. Good luck to you today, Carl."

"You too," he returns.

I push off of his boat, fire up the big motor, and idle out into the growing crowd. I'm excited, but admittedly a little nervous. The competitors–each in their high-tech, sparkly boats–emit a buzz, an energy, that I can feel in my guts. Most move around unsettled, eyes darting about anxiously. It's nearly unanimous that most would love to win today, but more than that, they just don't want to be embarrassed. It seems like no time has passed when suddenly, daylight is deemed safe for travel and the boats begin to line up for the single-file launch based on the numbers they drew at the pre-tournament meeting last night. Suddenly, the noisy field goes silent as all motors are cut, everyone stands, and hats are held over hearts for a recording of our national anthem amplified by a bullhorn. When that's finished the tournament director makes a few last-minute announcements.

"At my mark, the official time will be 5:58. And...mark. Now let's be safe out there today."

Motors are re-fired, as 140 small white puffs of two-stroke exhaust drift across the water.

"Boat Number 1!" the director calls. Arms wave in a boat near the front of the pack. "Gotcha Boat 1," he confirms, and boat one roars to life headed to its first spot. "Boat Number 2!" he continues. I watch this process repeat 75 times today, while I ease toward the front edge of the shrinking pack until it's my turn. "Boat 76!" he calls.

"Right here!" I wave.

"Thank you, 76," he confirms.

I scoot my glasses up the bridge of my nose, hang my hat on the boat's gearshift, sit up straight, check for other boats and push my HotFoot throttle to the floor. The nose of the boat points momentarily skyward, until the high-performance motor lifts most of the hull out of the water and levels her stance. Then she begins accelerating hard.

What was a calm glassy surface a few minutes earlier has been whipped into a washing machine froth from the 75 boats ahead of me. Although I'm a careful driver, the next few minutes are going to be a bumpy ride. I'm really not going to let off the throttle much as the boat jumps, lurches and rocks across the jumbled waves. These boats have a small windshield in front of the driver, but unless you duck right down behind it, the wind rushes by like a tornado, making it nearly impossible to hear and forcing my eyes to water cold streaks of tears across my temples. I visually follow the bubble trails and widening V-shaped wakes, to the white rooster tails of water spraying from the boats I'm chasing. Gradually, I overtake the first boat ahead of me, but before I can feel too cool about myself, a real hotrod blows by both of us like we're standing still. It looks like his prop is the only thing in the water. I'm pretty sure I could see daylight under his whole boat. Part of me says he's crazy, but most of me thinks that was awesome. I remind myself it's not a boat race, but I sure wish I had a boat like that.

Soon the field starts to thin as my competitors reach their starting spots. The backwater slough I'm headed for is coming up on my right. There's only one boat ahead of me that could still potentially be headed to my spot. I breathe a sigh of relief as he continues on, passing the turn. I know there are still dozens of other boats that started far enough ahead of me that I couldn't see where they went, but this time it looks like I'll get to start where I planned without anyone else's company.

As I ease off the throttle, the back end of the boat dips down, sending the nose skyward, until we lose enough momentum that the entire hull levels back into the water. Instantly the world changes from mayhem to tranquility. Red-winged blackbirds and leopard frogs call out in the distance. A gentle fog swirls and rises off the calm, smooth surface of the water. The wake from my boat moves out in all directions, causing a row of cattails to sway gently in unison–a fading reminder of the technology and machinery that only moments ago had been hurling us at 70 mph down the river. As I idle the last few yards to my starting point, the voice in my head is chattering non-stop. *I'm so glad that no one else is on this spot. Wait, why isn't anyone on this spot? Did I miss something else in practice? I'll bet the big bite is on the main river. I knew*

I should have spent more time checking that out in practice. I did catch fish back here, but that was late afternoon. Will they bite here first thing in the morning? That guy in the white Ranger had four rods with crankbaits on his front deck. I'll bet he's out on the main river–probably fishing wing dams. I did catch fish back here though. This style suits me better anyway. I'm not a great crankbait fisherman. I remember a day in the early fall two years ago when my buddy and I tore them up on crankbaits. Maybe, if this doesn't work out back here I can hit the main river next. I've got a great wing dam that I caught them on last year.

I turn the key and the big motor falls silent. In one swift movement I unzip my life preserver, make my way to the front deck, and deploy the trolling motor. Ten yards ahead of me the calm is broken as a bass chases some baitfish to the surface of the water. *I knew they were here!* cries the noisy voice in my head. I love this point in time. Right now, before I make that first cast, anything can happen. It doesn't matter how the fishing was yesterday. It doesn't matter how this tournament went last year. Right now, I can only assume everything could go my way. This day still has every possibility to be great. This could be the best day of fishing I've ever had. This could be the day I catch the biggest bass of my life. *God, just don't let me be skunked.*

Ch 2
The Real World

The alarm is set for 6 a.m. Two go-rounds with the snooze button and now it's 6:20.

"William," groans Trixie, still mostly asleep. "You're going to be late."

"Mmmm," I respond, sort of, but I just can't seem to move. God, I hate Monday mornings. Gone is the freedom and fresh air that the weekend brings. Back to the fluorescent-lit, coffee-fueled way I provide for my family. I guess I don't hate being a programmer analyst. I don't even hate the staffing company I've worked for the past nine years. I'm just so uninspired. Hey, I know a lot of people who'd love any job at all, so I'm not complaining. It's just that...

"Bi-ill!" she groans. I know when she uses my short name but still makes it two syllables, she's really getting annoyed. "You're going to be..."

"Late. I know, I know." I struggle to kick the covers off and swing my legs over the side of the bed. My feet slap the cold, unforgiving hardwood floor. Ugh, what a horrible contrast to the warm fluffy comforter I just left behind on the bed. I summon all my strength, fighting every urge I have to flop back down and call in sick...and slowly...I rise. Alright. Not so bad. Still time for a quick shower, and if I catch all the lights I should make it to the office on time.

I check myself in the mirror as I finish the last few buttons of my casual, collared, work appropriate shirt. Probably should have shaved but that will have to wait until tomorrow. Oh man, look at my sunglass tan from the weekend. I look like a raccoon. Ha! Fine with me. I wear my fisherman's tan with pride. Actually, I secretly feel it might give me more credibility as a big-shot fisherman among my coworkers and other civilians. I realize they

9

don't actually care about my patchy tan or know anything about competitive fishing, but at least they know I go fishing a lot. I must be good at it. I know it's ridiculous, but it gives people who don't really know me, something we can talk about. I click the bathroom light off and head down the hallway toward Dacey's room. I peek my head into the doorway, and catch her rolling over pretending to be asleep. I'm sure she's still sleepy, but I'm pretty sure she is technically awake.

"Good morning, sweetheart," I call out gently in a singsongy sort of way. I wait in the dim glow of the hall light for a beat or two. *Committed to her acting,* I think to myself. "Dacey. Wakey, wakey."

"Mmmm," she responds, sort of.

"I have to run, kiddo. Are you going to get up?"

"I'm up, Daddy. Have a nice day. Love you."

"Love you too. Mommy will be up in a minute to get you ready for school. Hey, please remind her that I'm going to Uncle Doug's after work for a while."

"Uncle Doug's? What for? Can I go?"

I've already taken a step away from her doorway. I stop. "We've got a tournament this weekend and we're going to get the boat and everything ready. No, not this time, Sweetie. I'll take you to visit Uncle Doug soon." I start hurriedly down the hall and call back over my shoulder. "I won't be too late. Love you, Dace."

I'm running toward the garage now. Alright, if I don't stop for coffee...ugh, I can buy coffee from the vending machine at work. Then as long as I don't get behind a school bus or garbage truck, I should be...I glance at the time on my iPhone... late.

Ch 3
The Plan

"How many beers should I pack for you?" Doug calls out as he walks into the garage carrying a large plastic cooler in front of him.

"You know I really don't drink much when I'm fishing," I answer from inside the boat, surrounded by fishing rods and lures. The truth is I really don't drink much anytime. I'm not opposed to drinking, but I just don't prioritize it anymore. I suppose my lack of enthusiasm for drinking is simply a side effect of getting older.

Doug stops and eyeballs me. "What kind of girly-man are you? How many should I pack?"

"Nice. I don't know. A couple per day will be fine," I cave. Obviously, his priorities are slightly different than mine. I want to make sure my tackle is in order before anything else. If we get there and I don't have any beer, I can deal with that. But if I hear from the locals that they've been crushing them on bone white Pop-Rs and I don't have a bone white Pop-R with me, I'll never forgive myself.

Doug stares at me just long enough to create an awkward moment, then, as if disgusted with me, says, "Alright then. That wasn't so hard, was it?" He's kidding.

Doug and I have a funny relationship. We fully respect, admire and enjoy each other's company, but we're always taking little shots at each other.

Doug fills the cooler and stows it in the back of his truck. He comes back into the garage with his mind finally on the tournament. "Oh, hey! Did I tell you I picked up a couple packs of those new creature baits from Berkley? Got 'em in pumpkin pepper and…" He stops and looks over both shoulders. Then he lowers his voice and whispers, "…solid black." His eyes dart around the room like he's double-checking for eavesdroppers.

"Very funny," I respond to his over-acting. He knows very well that I hold solid-black soft plastics as one of my closest-guarded fishing secrets. I went to the Bassmaster Classic tournament when it was in Chicago in 2000. The wind kept a lot of guys from venturing out into Lake Michigan, so they were fishing in the river and harbors right in town. We were walking around, watching guys from the bike path on Lake Shore Drive. At one point we were on a bridge over the Chicago River and Gary Klein was fishing right below us. I really pay attention to the details and I noticed that the jig he was pitching was solid black with a black trailer. Not black and blue, just black. Then I saw on the deck of the boat he had a tube and a Senko rigged up, both solid black. That's the kind of thing I notice. It's not a typical color choice, so there must be something to it. Gary Klein has won a lot of money fishing tournaments. Actually, not that particular tournament, but still. Gary Klein knows what he's doing. After that, I started using more solid black and I think it helped. Not many guys know about it. Doug knows. He also knows that we've caught quite a few fish in our time on solid-black soft plastics. He kids me about it, but I'll bet he'll be throwing solid black this weekend. "Let me see one," I say to Doug.

He reaches into the tackle locker and produces a bulging Gander Mountain bag. After a few seconds of rummaging through his new toys, he finds the pack and tosses it to me.

I pop the Zip-Lock seal and reach for one as the familiar wave of PowerBait odor hits me square in the nose. I breath in deeply. My wife hates the smell. My daughter thinks it's gross. I agree that it stinks, but I absolutely love it. That smell makes a connection deep in my brain that lets me know it's time to fish. That smell equals good times.

I hold the creature bait in front of my face like a jeweler inspecting a diamond. Basically, it looks like a super-muscular crayfish with a menacing scowl on its face–funny because real crayfish don't have faces. "I really like how thick the claws are," I inform Doug.

"And the body is big enough for a 5/0 hook, without it tearing out every cast," he points out enthusiastically.

"Mmmm," I nod in agreement. "But not too big. Nice and compact." I lay it flat in my palm to look at it from a different angle. "Good-looking bait," I announce, then tuck it back into its re-sealable bag and motion that I'm going to toss it back to him.

"Keep it," Doug says. "I got that bag for you. I knew you'd like 'em."

"Seriously? Wow, thanks. Well, what do I owe you?"

"Seriously?" Doug asks sarcastically, with one eyebrow raised. "We're good."

"Well, thanks. I think these could come into play this weekend. Hey, have you had a chance to call that guy with the cabin there? Did he give you any ideas as to what they're biting on?" The big pros aren't allowed to get help from the locals, but in a tournament at this level there are no rules against it, thank God.

"I did talk to him, but he says he hasn't been out much lately," Doug informs me.

"Too bad. He really used to know that stretch of the river," I lament.

"Yep. But he did say his neighbor has been whackin' some giant smallies on that big closing dam by the power plant. He said the only thing the guy ever uses is a white twin-tailed grub on a little 1/4-ounce jig. But the trick is..." Doug knows I'm very interested, so he pauses to add ridiculous drama. "...he dips the tips of the grub in chartreuse dye." Doug raises, then wiggles his eyebrows confidently, knowing this is exactly the kind of report I'm looking for.

"Nice work, Dougy!" I confirm, digging to the bottom of a tupperware container looking for twin-tailed grubs. "I'm really looking forward to this tournament. With a little luck, maybe we can win this thing."

"Let's do that," he agrees, and offers up his fist. I'm not typically a "fist bump" guy. I would never initiate, but in this case my brother-in-law has earned it. I lightly, but exaggeratedly punch his fist.

"Boom," he says as if it's the coolest thing ever.

Ch 4
Trixie

Well that was productive, I think to myself as I pull my truck into the garage. *I'm really looking forward to this tournament.* Van Halen's *Ice Cream Man* is playing on the radio, so of course I leave the engine running until the song ends. I know I own the CD and I've heard it a million times, but still–Van Halen. "...guarantee-ee-ee-ee-ee-ee-ee-eed...to...sat-is...fy." I turn off the key, unlock my seatbelt and lean into my door. Immediately I recognize the smell of good home cooking, even out here in the garage. "Oooh! I'll bet that's meatloaf!"

I rush through the door connecting the garage to the house, which happens to come in just off the kitchen. I breathe deeply. "Mmm, and that's homemade bread!" And there stands Trixie, the love of my life, just about to pull a square of plastic wrap over a plateful of food.

"You're home?" she questions, sounding surprised. "I thought you'd be late if you were going to Doug's. Did you go? Did you eat? Are you hungry? I made meatloaf."

She tends to ask a lot of questions. "I did go. I have not eaten. I am hungry. Yes, please."

"Oh, good," she says. "I was just wrapping up a plate for whenever you did get home. Actually, everything is still warm. We just ate. Would you like me to make you a strawberry Quick milk to drink, dear?"

"You read my mind." I pull up a seat at the breakfast bar in the kitchen and Trixie slides the plate across to me. "This looks great, hon! Thanks!" I praise her. She has accused me of taking her for granted on many occasions, so I've been making a real effort to keep the peace.

"So how's my baby brother?" she asks.

"Good. You know, typical Doug," I tell her over the sound of the spoon clinking around in the glass of Quick she's stirring. "He talked to one of the guys who lives right on the river and we got a pretty good tip–real 'locals only' stuff!"

"Oh that's nice," Trixie says. Was that sarcastic, I wonder? But I have no reason to believe she's being anything less than supportive. Maybe it's my own guilt that causes me to hear things that aren't actually there sometimes. "Boy it would be great if you guys actually won," she adds. Now what was that supposed to mean? Nope, nothing. We have our share of disagreements, but overall I'm happy to have her.

Actually, I met Trixie at a fishing tournament. I had signed up for the Monster Mash Open, a small tournament hosted by a bass club a couple pools south of me on the river. They called it the Monster Mash because they held it at the end of October every year, and because that late-fall bite can really produce some monster bags. Just for fun, the people who volunteered to work the tourney dressed up in Halloween costumes. Participants were encouraged to dress up too, but usually only a couple of the guys from that club actually did. For as silly as it sounds, this tournament drew a pretty strong group of competitors with some really good local sticks fishing it every year. I think its popularity was mostly because it was post-regular fishing tournament season and pre-deer hunting season. Everyone was looking for one last competition before our harsh Upper Midwest winter shut us down for the next five months.

So, my partner and I struggled a bit that day, arriving at the scales with only three keepers, instead of the allowed limit of five. It was a real shame because we started the day with a nice kicker–4 pounds, 15 ounces, I believe. I really thought things were finally going our way, but after a few more small keepers the bite shut down. So anyway, I remember standing in line with our bag of fish. As we approached the scale, I was shocked to see Cinderella was manning the bump board. *Who is that?* I thought, followed by, *Man, I wish we had five. I don't want to hand her my stupid three fish. We do have that good one, but still. Maybe I can explain to her that...*

But it was too late late. "Boat number?" she asked sweetly.

"Seventeen, princess," I responded. *Wow! Where did that princess thing come from? Hmm. As long as I didn't sound creepy that wasn't bad.* I wasn't typically very smooth with the ladies. I held my breath and started to prepare my apology. She looked confused for a split second, then remembered her costume...and smiled like an angel. I hoisted our catch into the utility sink they used to measure and stage fish. She grabbed the bag and poured out our short limit. The fish splashed into the bottom of the basin as the water disappeared through a hose fastened to the drain hole.

"There's a nice one!" she said encouragingly.

"Yep. Thanks. Things started off good. I'm not sure what went wrong. Lots of pike!" *Ugh, nice work. I'm sure the pike story will impress her, William. Honestly, I don't think if I had a 25 pound sack, that a woman like her would be impressed with me. Wow, I'm glad I didn't say that out loud. Just look at her,* I thought. I could tell right away that even beyond her costume, she was literally pretty as a princess. And she grabbed and measured the flopping bass without a hint of hesitation. I didn't know who she was. She must be taken.

"I've heard that a lot of people were catching pike today," she offered, "but I think this bass you got is the biggest I've seen so far."

"Really? Well, let's hope it holds up." She smiled and handed me my bag of fish.

"Good luck," she said, as the tournament director, who was dressed like Edward Scissorhands, called us to the scale.

But I didn't want to leave the princess. "Love your costume," I said over me

17

shoulder as my partner pushed me toward Scissorhands. "Sure wish I had worn my Prince Charming outfit," I called back in an uncharacteristically bold way. She smiled brightly and turned away to help the next team in line.

Well, sure enough, we were in contention for big bass that day. The $300 prize would just about bring us up to even for the weekend. As we waited anxiously for everyone to weigh in, I found myself sneaking glances at Cinderella every chance I got. Who was she? Should I have been nervous that someone was going to notice me watching her and get all defensive? Of course she must have been married to someone there. Certainly she wasn't there on a Saturday afternoon because of her love of measuring fish.

"Doug Pratt's sister," my tournament partner, Dan, announced as he aproached through the crowd.

"What? Who?" I demanded clarification.

"Doug is one of the members of the host club, and she's his sister. She's just here as a favor to him."

I hadn't asked my partner to go on this recon mission, but I'm sure he had noticed how I hadn't stopped looking at her. It was probably strange that I hadn't been talking about our pending big bass prize.

I considered this new information for a second. "Is she... ?"

" ...single," he finished my sentence. "She's only here because she's helping her brother out."

"Really?" I felt my stomach flutter a little. I had been imagining what I might say to her if I thought there was any chance for me, but now I might actually have a chance. Now I was going to have to act on it. I was pretty sure she was out of my league, but she hadn't given any indication that she thought so. I mean, I'm not ugly, I laughed to myself. I wasn't going to get any jobs modeling underwear or anything, but I was at least average. No, better than average, maybe. There had been attractive girls who'd liked me in the past. I was tall. I worked out. I was in pretty good shape. I took care of myself. I had a good job. And women told me I was nice. Ugh, I hoped she wasn't into the bad boy type, cause I...

"At 4 pounds, 15 ounces, big bass today goes to the team of Bill Buckner and Dan Simms," a voice announced over the P.A. There was a smattering of applause as my partner nudged me toward Edward Scissorhands. I snapped back to reality and we headed toward our $300 payday.

"Congratulations, gentlemen!" Edward offered his bladed hand and I shook it carefully. I could see Cinderella over his shoulder off to the side of the stage. She was watching! "So how did you get that big one today?" he asked, shoving the microphone in my face.

"Um, white spinnerbait," I lied. Hey, we caught the other two on spinnerbaits, but the big one was our secret.

"Spinnerbait," the MC repeated. "Was she shallow or deep?"

"Shallow," I replied. Really, I just wanted my check and I wanted to get off the stage. I still had to formulate a plan before the clock struck midnight and Cinderella slipped away.

"Great! Well thanks for fishing with us today, Bill... "

"It's William," I corrected him and made eye contact with the princess.

"Alright, William and Dan. Congratulations and if you wouldn't mind, go see Trixie, I mean Cinderella, when you leave the stage. She's taking pictures of all the winners for us today."

"Trixie!" the voice in my head shouted. I would gladly go see Trixie!

We walked down the stairs on the side of the stage towards the smiling princess.

"Congratulations," she offered. "If you two wouldn't mind standing together right there in front of our sponsor's banner, I'd love to get a picture for our newsletter."

"Of course," I smiled, more nervous than confident. I was trying to tell myself to be cool, but I'm pretty sure I looked nervous.

"Hold the check up a little higher, and..."click"...got it. Thank you, gentlemen."

"Our pleasure," I assured her.

She set down her camera and picked up a pen. "Now, it's Bill..."

"Yes, William actually," I quickly, but politely, corrected her.

"OK. William Buckner and Dan Sullivan," she wrote in her notebook. Then she smiled courteously. We all stood smiling in silence until it became obvious our business here was done.

"Um, do you need any other info?" I asked somewhat desperately. "Contact info or anything...you know...for your newsletter?

She looked puzzled. Dan rolled his eyes at me from behind her back.

"I mean, I could give you my phone number...you know, if you had any use for it."

Her expression changed. It warmed. "Yes. Why don't I take that down," she agreed.

Then she tore a piece of paper out of the notebook and handed it to me. "Here. You had better take my number as well...in case you have any questions...like when the newsletter is coming out...or anything." She smiled sweetly.

I guess Trixie has always made it easy for me. I smile at her as she watches me devour the meatloaf. "Thanks, dear. This is really delicious," I tell her sincerely.

"I know meatloaf is one of your favorites. I'm glad you're home in time to have it while it's still warm."

"Mmm, hmmm," I agree while chewing greedily. "This should be a good weekend," I steer the conversation back toward fishing. "I always enjoy fishing with your brother, and this is one of my favorite parts of the river." She notices that I have finished my bread and cuts me another slice. "Plus, the last club qualifying tournament of the year is on the same pool the week after next." I take a big gulp of my strawberry milk. When I lower the glass, I see that her face has changed. She looks...I don't know...hurt. "Everything okay?" I ask, and wipe my mouth with a napkin. She seems hesitant to respond.

Finally she speaks. "How long will you be gone for that one?"

"Well, that's a two-day because it's the last one of the year. I'll leave Thursday after work so I can practice on Friday, and then I'll leave after weigh-in on Sunday. It's not too long of a drive, so I should be home by around 6:00–7 at the latest." I stop speaking and study her face. No change. "Is everything okay?" I ask again.

"It's just that...well, if you're going to be gone, I guess it doesn't matter."

I put my fork down and push my plate away. "C'mon dear. What doesn't matter?" I plead.

"Well...I thought we had plans that Saturday. Remember, it's my cousin's

21

birthday? We're supposed to be going out for dinner with her and Connor, and their neighbors, the couple we met at their barbeque. Remember?" She doesn't sound mad. She speaks slowly and evenly. But actually, that's how I know she is mad. And, mad probably isn't the right word either. Hurt and disappointed is more accurate. I certainly don't try to hurt her. It's just that this is the last tournament of the club season and I'm right on the bubble going into this one. If I can put together a good showing, I'll make the six-man team and fish the regional. The top 12 from regional go to state. A good finish at state sends you to nationals. At nationals, the best finisher from each region fishes in the Bassmaster Classic. Seriously, the Bassmaster Classic! That's the tournament everyone on the water dreams of. Granted, it's a long shot, but someone will be going. And I know for sure it will not be the guy who's missing tournaments to go to a distant cousin's birthday dinner. Seriously, do adults really care about their birthdays? Trixie watches patiently, knowing I'm sorting it all out in my head. Is it me? Am I wrong here?

Ch 5
Never According To Plan

"Net!" I announce clearly and excitedly to Doug.

"Good one?" he asks as he reels in quickly.

"Feels pretty good," I inform him. Then we both watch a 4- to 5-pound smallmouth take to the sky with my twin-tailed grub dangling from the corner of its mouth. "Giant! Giant! Net! Net! Net!" I blurt out with increased enthusiasm. *God, I love this sport!*

In a flash Doug is next to me with the net poised and ready. "That's what we're looking for, buddy! Nice and easy!" he coaches me. "Did you see that beast?"

"Did I see him? How could I miss him? Just be ready with that net!" I say with a mixture of joy and panic in my voice. Suddenly, the fish turns and my 12-pound-test fluorocarbon line slices through the water like a laser beam. I reel furiously to keep up with him as he heads right toward the boat. "Be ready, Doug. Here he comes!"

Doug holds the net just above the surface, ready to scoop the fish that will greatly impact our fate today. The white grub emerges in front of us, but the bass is gone.

"Whaa." I make an empty, windy, guttural noise like I had just been punched in the stomach. I would prefer a real punch to what I had received. Just as quickly as it started, it was over. "What happened?" I ask rhetorically. Doug's shoulders slump down as he falls from his ready position. He drops the net into the bottom of the boat and returns to his spot on the back deck. I can't move. My mouth hangs open.

"That's alright. If there's one, there are more," Doug tries, but we both know. He makes a cast and tries to shake it off.

"What happened?" I ask again, still not really expecting an answer. "I didn't even feel him come off."

"Sometimes they just come off," Doug consoles me. "It looked like you did everything right. Sometimes they just come off."

I shake my head and swing the bait into my hand for inspection. Everything seems fine. The hook is straight and sharp. I feel sick. *Why does this always happen to me? That was a big fish for this stretch of water.* I drop the rod carelessly to the deck. *Man, I'd love to catch a break some day. I guess starting our day with a five plus in the box would be too much to ask.* I remove my hat, tip my head back, and slowly run my empty hand trough my hair.

"Hey, William! We're just about into the rocks back here!" Doug warns and I snap back to consciousness.

Alright, I'm awake now, but I'm pissed. I stomp on the trolling motor pedal just in time to hear the sick grinding sound of my skeg and/or prop dragging and scraping along the rocky bottom. "Perfect!" I pout. "What else is new?"

"Don't beat yourself up, William," Doug suggests. "We've still got all day. Let's re-focus and get back on 'em."

He realizes I am likely to be inconsolable for at least the next several minutes, but he knows he has to say something. I realize he's right, but I feel like I deserve a few minutes to feel bad. That fish was huge. I'm entitled to my recovery time. The memory of the big bass jumping replays again and again in my head. *Why me?*

Alright. C'mon William, I say to myself. I know I can't catch them if I don't have a lure in the water. I look at the collection of rods piled up at my feet.

24

The solid black, stick bait that Doug custom poured for me back when he was trying to start his D-Licious Bait Company, catches my eye. That's been my lucky, go to for a lot of years. Then I remember that we have some local insider info. Plus, I should probably stick with the bait that big fish just bit. I push my thumb down on the bar, flick my wrist, and send my white grub out to the upstream side of the rocky closing dam.

"Let's do this," Doug says, relieved to see me fishing again.

"Let's do this," I repeat. "But that last one is gonna sting for a while. I just don't understand why..." Then I realize my line is moving the opposite direction of the current. The tip of my rod is high–out of position for a good hookset. Quickly, I wind as much slack out of the line as possible and set awkwardly over my shoulder. The rod loads up for a split second, then the line goes limp. "God damn!" I say, as if trying to alert God to the injustice he is serving upon me. "Unbelievable! That was one, right there! Good one, too!" Honestly, I have no way of knowing the size of the fish that just bit.

"That's alright," Doug reminds me. "They're here, for sure. Just keep fishing."

Silently and disgustedly, I reel in my lure and check my hook, hoping to find something to blame. My posture and attitude is that of a man who's been wronged. That's two misses. The person who wins a tournament doesn't get two misses during the course of the day. You must pay attention and capitalize on every opportunity if you want to win.

"...never mind then," Doug says defensively. Then I hear splashing.

"What? Never mind, what?" I ask.

Doug swings a fat 16-inch smallmouth bass onto the carpet between us. "I said net, but you didn't respond, so I guess I'll just take care of it myself."

He works the hook from its jaw and holds it up for inspection. "Two and a quarter?" he asks for my opinion.

"Yeah. I'd say that's about right. Nice work, partner," I offer.

"Thanks, partner. And as long as we're on the subject, we're going to need to work as a team to have a chance." He says it with just the right tone to get me to stop feeling sorry for myself.

"You're absolutely right," I tell Doug as he digs in the tackle compartment for a cull tag.

"I hope I get to let you go by the end of the day, little guy," he says to his fish. I'm relieved to have something in the livewell, but Doug is probably right. We're going to need better than 16-inch fish to have a shot at this thing.

Having that first keeper in the box is amazingly calming, but I'm struggling to not think about how that two pounds could be 12 pounds. I've heard the big pros talk about dealing with loss. It's part of fishing. Maybe it gets easier over time, but it's not easy for me right now.

I stand up straight, plant my foot firmly on my trolling motor pedal and guide the nose of the boat into optimal casting position for both of us. It's still early. The sun won't peek over the trees for another 45 minutes or so. We have this local hot spot to ourselves and the fish are definitely here. Plus, we're using the super-insiders only, top-secret lure. That really should be enough to get the job done today. Then I see the spot where I last saw that big fish jump with my lure, and I feel the frustration washing over me again.

* * *

Doug's smallmouth weighs exactly 2-pounds, 5-ounces. We stand in the crowd and watch the other competitors bring their bags to the scales. It looks like a lot of teams are falling short of their limit today, but I'm not finding this information to be as comforting as I had hoped. There are a handful of other teams who went out on the same water, under the same conditions, and brought in huge bags of fish. In fact, most of these teams are always on

26

top at the end of the day–the white Ranger guy, Carl; Anthony Martins and Dr. Burke...I think his first name is Joe or Jack or something with a "J" (those guys have enough money to have all the latest equipment); and then there's Cam Seavers, and anyone he fishes with. He seems to go through partners pretty regularly. Man, I'd love to fish with him, because it almost guarantees a good finish. I've approached him a couple different times over the years in an effort to create a friendship. He's been civil enough, but I haven't really figured out an angle that clicks with him. I wonder what it is about all those guys that makes them so lucky? I mean, I know they're all experienced and skillful, but every time? I have to figure out what I can do to improve my luck.

Nearly everyone is in and it looks like five fish at just a hair under 20 pounds is going to be the winning weight today–Seavers and his partner. They are standing right next to me and Doug, waiting for the official results, so I decide to see what I can find out.

I lean into their personal space. "Hey, Cam. You guys tear 'em up today?"

"Hey, Bill. Yeah, we had a pretty good day."

"It's William," I interject.

"Sorry, William old buddy. How'd you guys do?" He notices my partner and tries to include him. "Hey, Doug."

Doug nods and replies, "Cam." Doug has never much cared for Cam. I think he might be a bit intimidated or jealous of Cam's track record.

"Tough day for us," I explain. "Man, I had a giant on all the way up to the side of the boat though. Probably would have been big bass for today." I recount the details for him, acting out the hookset with my invisible fishing rod. "Then it just came off."

"Oh, man. Tough break," Cam offers.

"Hey, sometimes it's just out of your control," I tell him, trying to sound as experienced and unphazed as possible.

"Yep," he agrees. "Still, tough break."

"So was the frog bite on for you guys today?" I inquire. I had seen him in a tournament here last month. He was fishing about 100 yards away from me throwing frogs across a big matted section. He won that day too.

"We caught 'em a lot of different ways today," he answers vaguely. Then I catch him make eye contact with his partner, who hasn't said a word. I would imagine Cam has sworn all of his partners to secrecy. There's a moment of awkward silence as it's obvious to all four of us that he has blatantly side-stepped my question. Cam chuckles nervously and spouts the old cliche, "I could tell you how we got 'em, but then I'd have to kill ya." He laughs heartily and the rest of us oblige.

Ch 6
A Revelation

I make my way down the long, cold, impersonal hall to the vending machines. Another Monday morning and I need caffeine.

I stand in front of the row of machines, wishing I was almost anywhere else right now. Coffee or Mountain Dew? Oh, that's right we don't get Dew here. Coffee or Mello Yello? Coffee it is. I feed three quarters into the slot, push the "Vanilla Mocha Dream" button...and nothing happens. Then I notice a new $1 sticker has been fixed over the old 75¢ sign. I sigh and dig into my pocket. The fact that I have another quarter with me feels like a small, sad victory. My change disappears into the slot and the machine springs to life. While pumps click on and off and my cup begins to fill, I wonder if they actually sell more coffee by naming it "Vanilla Mocha Dream" compared to "Coffee with Vanilla"?

"You gonna take your coffee, Buckner?" a voice from behind me snaps my mind back to reality.

"Oh...um, yeah." I grab my cup of steaming vanilla goodness and turn to face Egan. Ian Egan. I don't report directly to him, but he is my superior. He's on the same level as my boss, except he's really kind of a jerk.

"Did you get enough sleep, guy?" he asks with a big stupid smile. He pauses for half a second, then laughs as if he just made a joke. "Huh?" He laughs some more. I think he's trying to be friendly or playful or something.

"Yeah. I'm good, Ian." I respond. "You know...Monday morning." I take my first step toward my get away.

"Case of the Mondays," he exclaims and laughs again at his non-joke.

"Hey, didn't you have a tournament this weekend?"

The only things Ian knows about me are that I am a Programmer Analyst and that I fish. He's one of those guys who loves small talk, so he always wants to talk fishing. Normally I'm always up for talking fishing, but he's also one of those guys that doesn't know he doesn't know everything.

"Yep. We were over at Wabasha."

"Oh, the river," he says. "What do you catch over there anyway?"

"It was a bass tournament," I tell him.

"Largemouth or smallmouth?" he asks.

"Both," I answer.

He pauses for a second thinking it over. I try to take a sip of my coffee but it's still too hot. "When I was a kid, we used to catch white bass over there. How about white bass?"

"Nope. Just largemouth and smallmouth for the tournament," I inform him.

"Boy, we used to catch a lot of white bass there. My uncle had a cabin on the Wisconsin side near Wabasha. We'd fish right from his dock. Boy, we caught 'em. Big ones too." He holds up his hands indicating a size much bigger than any white bass I have ever seen. "Then my uncle would clean 'em up, and we would have them for lunch. You ever have white bass?" He doesn't wait for my answer. "It's no walleye, but I'll tell ya what...not bad."

"It's a great area to fish," I agree. I've taken several steps backwards as he's been talking, but he's been stepping with me.

He's been smiling and laughing the whole time, but suddenly his face lights up an extra degree or two. "We should go fishing out there sometime. With the two of us, I'll bet we could put a hurt on some old white bass."

"Sure. I go out there all the time. We should do that," I respond with as much enthusiasm as I can muster. I don't have any reason to be rude, and I'm pretty sure he'll never follow through on it.

"That sounds great!" he exclaims.

"Great," I echo. I turn and take a few steps toward the hall.

"Say, how did the tournament go?" he calls.

I stop and turn back around to face him. "Not like I hoped," I lament. "We only ended up weighing in one fish. It was terrible, really."

"One fish?" he questions. "I thought you were a big-time fisherman."

Great! Now he's going to question my abilities. I feel like I need to explain what happened–let him know that I am able to catch them. We just had a few bad breaks. I take a breath. "Fact is, I started the day with a giant smallie." I hold up my hands to indicate the size.

"Really!" he replies, sounding impressed.

"I saw him jump clear out of the water. Then he rushed the boat." I do the best reenactment possible with my coffee in one hand and my invisible rod in the other. "Just as my partner was about to net him, he just came off. Nothing I could do." That aught to convince him of my fishing prowess. I was just unlucky, but I could get on the big fish.

"Just came off?" he says with more delight than I expected. "You had the game-winning fish, and you flubbed it?" he asks as he starts laughing.

"Yeah, not so funny when it happened," I chuckle politely. Really I'm steaming at his reaction, but I think this might be over more quickly if I just play along.

But his laughter only gets louder. "Let me see if I got this straight," he continues, "Bill Buckner flubbed an easy play that cost him the big game? Do you see the irony in that?" He laughs hard. "Bill Buckner!" More laughter.

"Good one," I say and turn to leave.

"That was a real game six for you!" he continues, but I don't respond. "Oh, come on, Bill. I'm just having some fun with you," he calls out as I drag my way back to my office.

I've been battling the Bill Buckner thing my whole life. The truth is my father did name me after the ballplayer. He's a die-hard Cubs fan. In 1977, the year I was born, Bill Buckner joined the team. My dad was so excited that he shared a last name with the new player, he thought it would be great if his son shared the whole name. I am William Joseph Buckner, just like the Major League ballplayer. Obviously, my dad had no way of knowing that despite his successes, Buckner would be best remembered for a single fielding error during game six of the 1986 World Series. I remember having bragged to my friends at school about how Bill Buckner, the guy I was named after, was playing in the World Series. Starting the day after game six, they teased me for weeks. Anytime anyone dropped anything, they would point and laugh. I have spent the rest of my life trying to get away from that name.

I sit at my desk and try to get my mind back on business. Down the hall I hear a sudden outburst of laughter–Ian's stupid laugh. Then there's a second and third laugh joining him. He's telling the story to everyone. I stretch my leg and push the door shut with my foot–perhaps the only advantage to having a super-small office. I pick up my hot coffee with both hands and hold it up to my mouth, but I don't tip it back. I just hold it there, close my eyes, and inhale the warm, soothing, vanilla flavored steam deep into my lungs. Slowly and calmly I picture all the horrible ways my fellow employees could meet their fates. Smothered by a dump truck full of white bass, perhaps? I smile to myself. I take another breath of coffee, hold it in for a second, then release it slowly and open my eyes. I've used this little ritual before. It's amazing how quickly I'm able to change my mood and get back to work. Now, lets see what's on the docket today. I tap the spacebar on my keyboard and my computer opens its eyes. 17 emails. I start with the messages from my boss, Greg. Specifically, I had better start with the one titled: WTF? "What could this be?" I wonder to myself.

> *William-*
> *I just don't understand how you were able to take care of that problem with the payroll program that quickly. How did you even know where to start looking for that line of code? You are either incredibly lucky or...nope, I'm going with lucky (winky smily face). But in any case, I just wanted to tell you thanks and*
> *nice work.*
> *-Greg*

"Lucky?" I smile. "He's lucky I don't resign," I think, imagining a winky smily face at the end of my thought. Greg and I have a really good working relationship. He's a good boss. We share a mutual respect and a similar sense of humor.

> *Reply:*
> *I'm not lucky, I'm logical. You're welcome.*

Logic really is the key to being a good programmer. If you put good information in, you get good information out. To be honest, sometimes I'm not entirely sure how I can see the problem and fix it so quickly. I think it's just a confidence thing. I get into the "zone." I know I will figure it out, so my brain just gets right to it.

I take another breath of coffee. Then I try a small sip, but it is still hotter than I like it. My mind wanders to the tournament for a second. Fishing is always somewhere near the front of my thoughts.

"I wish I could see the answers that quickly when I'm fishing," I lament. *Why can't you?* the voice in my head answers itself. *Seriously? Is that the difference between the consistently high finishers and the 'also rans'? If the simple key to success as an analyst is applying logic and confidence, would the same thing work for fishing?*

My computer screen switches to power saver mode and I can see myself clearly in the dark, shiny glass. I stare at my reflection and consider the question I just asked. *The logical answer is...yes.* Well, now this is getting exciting!

I smile and take an extra deep breath of my coffee. I could really go for a sip but it's still too hot. How long ago was I in the break room? Then I think about Ian again. "Ugh, Ian." Good thing I've figured out a great way to forget about him. It would be great if I could permanently forget him, but at least this way I can get back to work. I pause and the image of the big bass jumping flashes through my mind, followed almost immediately by an intense reoccurrence of the frustration I felt. I realize that it feels a lot like dealing with Ian.

Oh man, William. You're on to something, here. Go with it. Run with it! So, if I'm able to use my coffee ritual to change my negative state at the office, would it work to change my state on the water? I sit up straight and smile. *The logical answer is...yes.*

Ch 7
A New Plan

For the rest of my work day I am a slightly less dedicated programmer. My mind works overtime on my new concepts. I do some Google searching and find very little on the idea of performance psychology as it pertains to fishing. Baseball? Sure. Golf? Absolutely. Olympiads? Tons. The idea that anyone would compete in any Olympic event without preparing mentally is apparently ridiculous. It has been an integral part of the Olympic training regimen for decades. I wade through volumes of information. I'm delighted to see how much of what I read would easily translate to tournament fishing. I read the U.S. Olympic Committee's Top Ten Guiding Principles for Mental Training and scribble the ideas that hit home with me on a small notepad I keep on my desk.

1.) Physical training and physical ability are not enough to succeed consistently. Mental training needs to supplement physical training for consistent success.

2.) A strong mind may not win an Olympic medal, but a weak mind will lose you one. Although mentally strong athletes do not always win medals due to a variety of conditions (e.g., health, training), athletes with a weak "mental game" virtually never win at the biggest competitions.

3.) Thoughts affect behavior. Consistency of thinking = consistency of behavior. Understanding and controlling the thinking process helps athletes control their behavior.

This is a real eye opener. It explains a lot about my so-so success rate. Sure, I've had the basic notion that I need to stay focused and positive during events, but I've never considered the idea that I should be practicing before I'm on the water.

And furthermore, where is this information? I can't be the first person to think of this! I have spent a relatively large percent of my life reading and researching what the bass fishing industry media offers up. Granted, I've learned a lot about new techniques, lures, colors and gear. I think you need to know these things, but now I realize I plateaued in my development as an angler a long time ago. I sit and wait for the next big secret to be revealed. I can catch them pretty well, but now that the...lets say Alabama rig, has been revealed I'll really start catching them. In the big picture, a new color of finesse worm, or a higher gear ratio reel, or even an Alabama rig, will not have nearly as much impact on my success as building a logical approach and a strong mind.

So why aren't there articles on mental performance in every issue of my favorite magazines? I take a sip of my afternoon vanilla coffee and ponder the question for a minute. Then it hits me–two reasons, really. The companies that manufacture these new products are the main advertisers in these magazines, TV shows and websites. They're also paying the salaries of the big pros who provide the content for the magazines. It's business. I can understand that. Plus, without strong sales of fishing products there would be less competition and less advancement.

I appreciate how the system works. I know first hand that the products I use now are light years ahead of the products I started my fishing career with. That explains why the media is mostly focused on products. The second reason for this lack of information is simply human nature. It's easier to understand how this new lure will catch more fish than to analyze how the touchy-feely, mental stuff will make a difference. It's tangible. I can see how nice that lure swims. I can feel how smooth this new 18-ball bearing reel is. It's also easy to find something to blame when things don't work out. "That guy beat me because he gets his lures custom made by the same guy that makes all the top-secret, custom lures for the big-shot pros." Or, "I can't afford that new 4D sonar system, so how can I compete?" I know as well as anyone that lures are very attractive to fishermen. They're fun to buy and collect, and somewhere in the back of my mind, I hope that this lure...this new lure...is the one that fish absolutely cannot resist!

I am pumped! This is a real breakthrough! I jot down a few more key points, tear the pages from my notepad and stuff them in my coat pocket. I check my e-mails and start wrapping up my workday. I can't believe I only have one more tournament before the end of the year. I'll do what I can this week and see if it makes a difference. The good news is I'll have all winter to research, study and train. Then I'll hit it hard next year. They're not gonna know what hit 'em! Then I remember a handful of my fellow competitors fish consistently and always finish in the money. Are they using the same mental techniques the golfers and Olympians use? What about the big pros? Are all of these people keeping this secret to themselves? Is this the biggest secret in fishing? Can I talk to Doug about this? Maybe I'll see how this next tournament goes. Ugh, I still need to decide and discuss with Trixie, whether I'll be able to fish that tournament. Birthday party for an adult? Really? Maybe I'll wait until I have some proof before I run it past Doug. After all, as my main tournament partner we should be on the same page. Oh God, we'll be a force next year! But I'm dying to talk to somebody about this. Trixie! I'll tell Trixie! I put my computer to sleep, grab my jacket and head for the exit. This is how every day of work should be, I smile to myself.

Ch 8
Home

I arrive home to find Trixie and Dacey halfway through Disney's *The Little Mermaid*. A crab with a Jamaican accent is singing about how great everything is "unda da sea!"

"Hi, dad!" Dacey jumps up and meets me at the door with a big hug.

"Hi, kiddo!" I say to the top of her head as I wrap her in my arms. It's amazing how this kid can make every care in the world disappear. "How was school today?" I ask.

"Fine," she responds. She does well in school, but she's not terribly enthusiastic.

"Just fine?" I ask with a playfulness in my voice. "What was the best thing that happened in first grade today?"

"Well, my friend Jennifer kept singing the song "Part of Your World" from this movie. So when I got home I asked Mom if we could watch it.

"You used to watch this one a lot when you were younger," I remind her. "It was your favorite."

"I know, Dad. But now I'm older," she says, rolling her eyes a little.

"Yes, you are," I agree. "But don't be in such a big hurry about it, please." I pat her head and she runs back to her spot on the floor in front of the TV. My eyes follow her and meet Trixie's eyes as she sits on the sofa.

"Hello, dear," she calls and blows me a kiss. "Did you have a good day?

Dinner will be ready in about a half-hour."

"Perfect. If you two don't mind I'm going to run upstairs and research something on my computer for a bit. Oh, and yeah, pretty good day." I hang my coat by the door and head toward the stairs. Then I remember my notes and double back to the coat. I hold up the small stack of papers and smile like a goof when I see that Trixie is watching me.

"I'll let you know when it's time to eat," she calls.

Stair number three squeaks a familiar and comfortable greeting as I go past. I like our house. It's not a mansion, but it's very comfortable. The third bedroom on the right is my home office...and Trixie's craft and sewing room. I know I've sat in front of a computer all day, but my home office is different. It's comfortable. The lighting isn't fluorescent. My chair is big and supportive. My portion of the room is decorated with artistic prints of bass, beautiful landscape photography, and the few small trophies I've won over the years. I fire up iTunes and hit shuffle. My taste in music is very diverse but leans toward 80s and 90s hard rock.

I remembered on my drive home, that I had read or heard somewhere that Rick Clunn was considered the Zen guy of the professional fishermen. I can't remember if it was an article he had written or maybe someone else had said that about him. What I know is he's had a long and successful career, setting lots of records along the way. I also know for sure he has a line of square-billed crankbaits with his name on them. I have three or four of them that I picked up after I saw him win an FLW tournament with them a while back.

I type "Rick Clunn Mental Performance" in my Google search window. Let's see. His Facebook page. A few sponsor pages referencing him. Hmm. Here's an old forum post from a guy wondering about Rick Clunn's Angler's Quest book series. That sounds promising, but it's an old link from about five years ago. Let's see.

"Has anyone read these books and are they worth it?" asks BassSlayer666. The answers vary, but most are positive. The responses that didn't like it say they just couldn't relate to all the Zen, tree-hugger hippie stuff. This sounds like a great place to start! I follow the link in the forum to the books, but the address is no longer valid. I search for the Angler's Quest series but can't find anyplace to buy them. Clunn has a Facebook account. Do I dare contact him directly? Oh, maybe eBay, I remember. Sure enough, someone in Clearwater, Florida is selling the entire series and the high bid is currently $20.01. I excitedly enter my bid, with plenty of padding. I want to make sure I get these books.

My search also reveals that Clunn had been featured in a critically acclaimed book titled *Bass Wars,* written by Nick Taylor in 1988. I hop over to Amazon and find it right away. In stock and just $12.95. Done!

Then to round out my research I decide on a book called *Mental Training For Winning: Accelerated Inner Game Secrets of Sport Psychology.* This is going to be a good winter, but I'm already eager to start next year's tournament season. I hear a gentle knock, but the door isn't even closed. I turn and find my beautiful, smiling daughter carrying a big glass of strawberry Quick.

"I brought this for you, Daddy. Mommy says dinner will be ready in five minutes."

I hop up and take the extra full glass from her slightly unsteady hands. "Thank you, Baby Doll! How was your movie? Good as you remembered it?"

"Good! Funny! I like Sebastian the Crab. And now I can remember the words so I can sing with Jennifer tomorrow!"

"That's excellent, Dace!"

I click my mouse and put my computer to sleep. I'm very encouraged about all my breakthroughs today. I sure hope I'm on to something here. It seems so logical.

I smile at my little girl. "All right! Let's go see what Mommy made us for dinner."

* * *

After dinner, Trixie does dishes while I get Dacey ready for bed. Our standard ritual includes brushing teeth, putting on pajamas and getting her all tucked in. I read one book to her, then she reads one book to me. Then she chooses one song that we sing together. Of course, tonight's song is "Part of Your World."

After that I meet Trixie on the sofa where she is reading a romance novel. She lowers the book as I sit down, favoring me with her smile.

"So you said you had a pretty good day at work?" she asks. My normal answer to that question is usually less enthusiastic and she picked up on it.

"Yes, but not because of my job," I clarify. "Today started out like crap, but then I had an idea...a revelation really."

"Oh?" she asks, encouraging me to continue, running her hand through her hair.

"I think I understand why I haven't had more success in tournament fishing. Actually, I still haven't confirmed anything, but it's all based on logic. Anyway, it turns out that almost every other sport applies mental conditioning practices to its top athletes. Golfers. Runners. Swimmers. Basketball players. They all incorporate psychological conditioning regimens as a part of their practice. I think that might be a big part of what's missing from my practice. I mean, I know how to catch fish. You've been with me in the boat. You've seen the volumes of fish pictures. The time I struggle is always during a tournament. Why is that?" I ask. I could feel myself really getting fired up about this.

"Interesting," she confirms, as she snaps her head causing her long, blonde hair to flip to one side.

"It is interesting," I agree. "The thing is, I think I may already have some of the skills I need. I just never thought to apply them to my fishing."

"How so?" she asks while fussing with her hair very deliberately.

"Like at work. When I'm analyzing a problem with a program, I just get into a zone. My confidence stays high and I perform well. I've created that confidence through hours of practicing and learning. At some point I just let it become automatic."

"That's true. You're very good at your job," she compliments me, then sighs in defeat realizing I'm probably not going to notice her new hairdo.

"Plus, I've actually been using a simple routine to eliminate the stress of my workplace and let me get back to my job quickly and positively."

"Really? How do you do that?" she asks.

"Remember, I told you about my coffee trick?"

"Oh, that thing where you sniff your coffee and go to your happy place?" I wish she hadn't made it sound so un-scientific, but I'm impressed she remembered. I nod enthusiastically.

"So, you'll always have a cup of hot coffee with you in the boat?" she asks with concern.

"No. Well, maybe. If that's what it takes. I'm not sure yet. I've ordered a couple books and plan to do some studying."

"That all sounds very interesting," she smiles enthusiastically.

"I've got all winter to get this figured out. I'll start training my brain, and next year will be awesome." I sit back with a big, satisfied smile and wait for her response. I've given her a lot of info, and I know she'll give me her honest feedback. I sure hope she doesn't tell me I'm crazy.

"That's great, honey," she assures me. "I really think you're on to something." I smile even bigger. Then suddenly, her smile fades and her face twists like she has a question. "Does this mean you're not planning to do that tournament next weekend?"

"The tournament next weekend!" the voice in my head shouts. I had forgotten all about it. I look at Trixie and she smiles hopefully. I think this new mind-frame could make a real difference, even by next weekend. If I can make the team next weekend, then I fish the regional next year. By next year, I'm pretty sure I'll be unstoppable. I look at her again. She waits patiently, knowing my brain is struggling to find an answer. I hate to hurt her, but this could be my big break.

"I'll tell you what," I finally answer. "It's a two-day tournament, but I think if I can have a good showing on Saturday, that might be just enough to get me on the team. I'll practice on Friday, fish Day 1 on Saturday, and be home by 6:30 so we can go to the birthday party."

"Really?" she asks excitedly, considering this thoughtful gesture to be much more important than not noticing her hair.

"Really," I confirm. "At least I'll have a chance to make the team. That's all I ask."

"Oh William, you're so good to me," she exclaims as she throws her arms around my neck.

I hug her back and realize that even if I don't win a fishing tournament ever, I really am a pretty fortunate guy...God, I sure hope I win a fishing tournament.

Ch 9
Just a Taste

Well, that was a pretty solid practice day I think to myself as I pull up to the dock. I probably would have weighed in about 15 pounds and I didn't even beat up any areas. As soon as I caught a decent fish or had several keeper bites, I left the area immediately. I have three different patterns working pretty well. I haven't seen anything in the weather or pool level predictions that lead me to believe tomorrow should be any different. Yep, I'm feeling pretty confident.

I received two of my new books earlier this week. I got a chance to study one pretty thoroughly, and skimmed the important points of the other. Although I didn't really have time to do any of the psychological training techniques, the concepts have given me a real boost. Just realizing that the way I control my thoughts will have a major impact on my experience is a big deal. Ideally, I would have a day where I wouldn't have to consciously reach into my new bag of tricks, but it's giving me a lot of confidence just knowing I have a plan in place.

I back my trailer down the ramp until my taillights disappear just under the surface of the water. As I've done a thousand times before, I use the big motor to ease my boat backwards away from the dock. I line the point of the nose up with the trailer winch and gently begin my approach. Then, just as the hull makes its first contact with the trailer's carpeted bunks, the boat shudders hard and there's a loud mechanical, banging noise as my prop hits something solid and immoveable under the water. Visibility in the river's murky depths is relatively low, so there's no way to confirm what I hit, but a quick inspection once I'm in the parking lot reveals some significant damage. There are several deep gouges on the blades of the prop, and the entire leading edge of one blade is folded forward. It's amazing how quickly this sort of thing can happen. I was driving about as slowly as the boat will go. I had the

45

motor trimmed up, but apparently not high enough. I spin the prop and watch closely. I can't tell for sure, but it looks like the shaft may be bent. I spin it again and focus hard on a dot in the center of the end of the prop shaft. If that center point moves as the prop spins, that's bad. I spin it again, hoping my eyes are playing tricks on me. I'm pretty sure it's bad.

I sort through the back deck storage compartment, and uncover my spare prop and the socket wrench I need to change it. Unfortunately, this only solves the smaller part of my problem. A bent prop shaft allows oil to leave the lower unit gear case while water replaces it. Without oil to keep the gears lubricated, I'm driving a ticking time bomb. Replacing a bent prop shaft is relatively affordable. Replacing a blown lower unit is thousands of dollars. Plus, my insurance will cover the repair now, but if driving it as is causes bigger problems, I'm on my own.

As I kneel on the rough gravel parking lot, and loosen the big nut that holds my old prop, I start to think about my plan for tomorrow. My favorite area from today's practice is about 20 miles upriver. The closest spot was about 12 miles. I think it would be risky, and frankly stupid, to even attempt the shorter run. The areas I liked were major secondary sloughs, not main river, but not far from it. Most of my fish were on the downstream ends of islands, especially if there were some logs and timber piled up on the break. I can picture a couple islands within a mile or so of the takeoff. I'll have to take a look at the map tonight and see if there's anything else that fits that description nearby. I'll just have to stay close and drive slowly. I'm sure I'll find some fish.

I slide the backup prop on, secure the big nut that holds it in place and give it a spin. Looks better from a distance anyway. Then I stop and stand up behind my boat. Suddenly it dawns on me that I am relatively unphazed by this tragic turn of events. Normally, I would have asked, "Why me?" Normally, I would have started practicing my excuse speech. Now, I just dealt with it and stayed focused on catching fish. My confidence is still surprisingly high. This could be the difference between the consistent finishers and everybody else. Maybe I'm fooling myself, but I can't wait for tomorrow.

I'd better get to the hotel. I'm meeting my partner at 5:00. We drew partners at the club meeting last week. I let them know that I wasn't going to be able to stay for both days. One of the younger guys, Dylan, said he was supposed to go to a football game with his girlfriend on Sunday anyway. Perfect. The club decided to just pair us up. He's a nice kid. Smart, enthusiastic about fishing, but has a lot of other things going on right now. I hate to disappoint him with the news of the boat, but sometimes these things are unavoidable. We'll still go fishing tomorrow. Everything will be fine.

* * *

I'm surprisingly calm, I think to myself as Dylan and I float just in front of the ramp, waiting for takeoff. Not having a specific plan takes a lot of pressure off. I know for a fact that nobody will beat me to my first spot–I don't have one. Plus, I'm not expected to do well today. I know it sounds weak, but I have a perfectly legitimate, built-in excuse if things don't go well today.

I make eye contact with Doug. He's riding along with Ben Winters. Ben is in the lead for Angler of the Year in the club. He's a good stick and a nice guy. I've heard he has a bit of a reputation for not giving his co-angler much of a shot, but sometimes that stuff can be exaggerated. He's always been cool to me. I'll wait and see what Doug has to say about his day before I make any judgements.

"Sucks about your prop," Doug calls out when they get close enough.

"Sorry to hear it, William. That really does suck," offers Ben.

"Thanks guys. These things happen," I respond. Then Ben launches into a story about cracking his lower unit at the state tourney with the winning bag of fish in the box. That reminds Doug of the time he got stuck on the wrong side of a lock with a 6-pound smallmouth and couldn't get back in time. Then Dylan remembers the time he saw bass pro Travis Manson beach his boat on a sandbar for two hours down by La Crosse.

"Cost him the tourney," Dylan finishes.

Fishermen all have hard-luck fishing stories. If you've been participating in this sport for any time at all you realize how quickly it can all go south.

"So how bad is it bent?" Ben asks turning the focus back on my immediate trouble.

"Not terrible, but it definitely needs replacing," I explain.

"Okay to run today, though?" Ben looks for clarification.

"Maybe, but I think we're just going to stay close. I'll probably just idle around."

"You know the first point here, just as you come out of this cove," he points over his shoulder, "is always good for a couple retreads."

By retreads he means fish that have recently been caught in other tournaments. It's pretty common knowledge that after the fish are released, they'll have a tendency to set up on the first acceptable spot and rest up for a couple days.

"Thanks, Ben. I've got a couple things in mind, but I imagine we will end up checking that out," I tell him.

Then I notice Doug is giving me the stink eye.

"What's with you?" I ask playfully.

"What's with you is the question," Doug states accusingly. He cocks his head to the side as if he's waiting for an answer. But he doesn't really wait, he continues, "You seem awfully chipper for a guy with a limping boat. I'm almost certain you didn't practice anywhere near here. What have you got cooking?"

"Nothing cooking," I raise my hands in defense. "I just figure there's plenty of fish within a one mile radius of this launch ramp. We're just going to go fishing and see what happens. I like going fishing." I pause and stare at him innocently as if waiting for an apology. When I know that I'm not getting one I continue, "It's OK if like to go fishing isn't it?"

Doug waits for me to finish, and squints as if he's studying me and thinking about what I just said. "Nope," he concludes. "I'm not buying this. Are you buying this?" he asks his partner in his mock rage. Both Ben and my partner, Dylan, have been chuckling at this faux heated exchange.

"Leave me out of this," Ben laughs.

"If you guys want to follow us around and keep an eye on us, you are absolutely welcome to," I inform Doug. "Or, maybe you could pull us over to your spots, Ben?" I raise my eyebrows at them.

Behind us the club tournament director announces that we're going to get started and calls for Boat 1.

Ben laughs at my suggestion. "You're on your own, William. I'm gonna trust you."

"Alright. If you're sure," I continue kidding.

"One hundred percent," Ben assures me and fires up his outboard. "Good luck to you guys today, William." His smile changes to a serious face. "Be safe. If you get in a bind, give Doug a call," he offers. "We're not going too far."

"Thanks, man. I'm sure we'll be fine, but thanks." I tip my hat to them. Ben puts the boat in gear and they start to move. "Tear 'em up today, guys," I offer. Then I make eye contact with Doug, and give him the "fake gun point" and a wink. He smiles and nods, and they pull away.

I fire up the big motor and find my way to the back of the pack. I've informed the tournament director that I'll go last. No sense getting in everybody's way. After a couple minutes it's just us and the director. He hops down from the front deck of his boat and gets into the driver's seat.

"Good luck to you guys today," he calls. Then he puts his boat in gear and takes off.

I turn my head to Dylan. "You ready?"

"Let's do this," he says enthusiastically and offers his knuckles for bumping. Again, not my thing, but I'm happy to oblige.

I put the boat in gear and at 6.2 miles per hour, we're off to just go fishing. It's a beautiful morning. Given the option, I'd rather be seeing it at 70 mph, but this really is a nice change of pace. I watch a great blue heron wading near shore as we idle by. Suddenly, he stops and plunges his long, pointed beak into the water near his feet. He shakes his head and emerges with what looks like a bluegill.

"That heron just got one!" I cry and point to the bird. "Everyone's catching them," I joke.

Beautiful day, I think to myself. But then I decide I should give this tournament more of my attention. I picture the circumstances that had worked for me in practice. What had I learned? What was I seeing here? Based on the current conditions, what makes the most sense?

We have been traveling for about 10 minutes. I pull up to a long, thin island that separates the main river from a backwater area. I can see a thin edge of submerged weeds a few feet from the shore with a handful of assorted trees and logs washed up against it. I turn to move closer and notice the bottom coming up quickly.

"If there's any depth in those trees, I think we're going to start here," I tell my partner.

"Looks good," he says excitedly.

The depthfinder says 3.8 feet under the boat. Probably a bit shallower in those trees. It depends on where the contour break is. Sometimes the current of the river can scour out deceptively deep areas right against the shore. There is some current here. Let's fish for a bit and see what we see. I quiet the big motor, climb onto the front deck, and deploy the stealthy, electric trolling motor.

One more quick analysis of the conditions, and I decide a buzzbait is the best choice to cover some ground and reveal any active fish in the area. I notice Dylan picks up a rod with a 6-inch Senko–black with a chartreuse tail. *Oh, man. That's a good call, I think to myself. I know they'll eat that thing. I wish that's what I had picked up. Would it be a jerky move to pick up my Senko rod now? Wait, wait, wait there, stupid voice in my head! Buzzbait is a good call. Your analysis is valid. Try not to be so easily distracted. Thank you rational voice,* I say to myself and smile at how insane that little exchange was. I wonder if everyone fights these same battles in their head?

I take a deep breath and zip a cast out parallel to shore just outside of the visible weed edge. A buzzbait is a great call for this situation–low light, shallow water, lots of cover. Plus, the bait moves at a constant, brisk pace so you can cover a lot of water, and it gurgles and clacks noisily along the surface, calling fish from a distance.

I'm moving the boat fairly quickly for now, until I can prove there are active fish in this area. The steady "Rrrrrrrrrrrrrrrrrr," of my bait is somewhat hypnotic. Quickly, I settle into a smooth rhythm. "Rrrrrrrrrr, Click. Zzzzzzzzzz. Splash". "Rrrrrrrrrr" and so on. As I'm casting, I'm trying to imagine what the world underwater looks like. I can only see the tip of that little limb sticking above the surface, but I try to imagine what the whole branch looks like underwater. What spot on that branch would make a good

51

ambush point for a hunting bass? Which direction will he be facing? I position my casts so my lure will come past the highest-percentage spots. If possible, I look for ways to allow my bait to travel through multiple prime spots in a single cast. Maximizing efficiency can pay off over the course of a tournament day.

My next cast lands just beyond a log that is anchored to the shore on one end. It sticks 15 to 20 feet out into the water at a 45-degree angle. I can see a small eddy formed behind it. My bait gurgles along the surface until it crashes into the face of the log. It struggles and bumps along the upstream face the last foot or so, until it clears the obstruction and buzzes free. But it only buzzes briefly, before a good, solid 3-pound largemouth surges from the slack water and crushes it!

"Net! Net!" I call to my partner.

Dylan is at my side in a flash and ready with the net. I throw 20-pound-test braid on my buzzbait rod, so the fight is pretty short-lived. He scoops the struggling fish cleanly, hands me the net, and gives me a solid pat on the back, as he heads back to his fishing rod.

"That'll work!" I shout enthusiastically. "Nice job with that net, partner! Thanks!"

"No problem. Good fish," he congratulates me.

I clip a cull tag in the bass' lip and quickly hang him on the scale before depositing him in the livewell.

"Three-one," I inform my partner.

I pick up my rod and we both start casting a little more intently than before. That was fun, I think to myself. "Click. Zzzzzz. Spalsh. Rrrrrrrrr. Gun-Doooosshhh!" Another hungry bass annihilates my bait.

Before I can call for the net, my partner acknowledges my fish with a "Holy crap!" as he drops his rod and heads for the front deck. "Nice work, William!" he yells as he scoops my second fish.

This one weighs in at three pounds even. I reunite him with his old buddy in my livewell and head back to the nose of the boat.

"Your turn, partner," I offer. Dylan is already back in the water doing everything he can to get his turn.

I assess the remaining stretch of shoreline. Not quite as many trees as this first bit, but I think we'll continue all the way around this island. We fish the next several minutes very focused, but without reward. As we round the point of the island, my intensity ratchets up a notch or two. I remember my success from yesterday's practice. My casts are zipping out effortlessly and my aim is flawless. I'm confident that each cast has every possibility to connect with another bass. "Click. Zzzzzz. Splash. Rrrrrrr. Click. Zzzzz. Splash. Rrrrrrrrrr."

We've fished our way past the point and now we're moving along the backwater side of the island. I can't see any visible wood along this shore. I notice that the shoreline is flatter and the bottom looks more mucky. The thin, defined strip of weeds from the river side has been replaced by much wider patches of weeds. In fact, the weeds nearest the shore are emergents like lily pads mixed with some arrowhead. This is definitely different than my spots from yesterday. Then I notice that it's another foot shallower back here. I'm losing that positive vibe. I think it might be time to get out of here and look for..."

"Here we go," my partner tells me with some enthusiasm in his voice. Quickly but smoothly he reels the slack out of his moving line, then rears back hard to set the hook. "Fish! Fish!" he cries, then adds, "Good one!"

A big green head shakes violently across the surface of the water, trying to dislodge the black Senko hanging out of its mouth. *Good one is right,* I think to myself as I hurry for the net. This fish is much bigger than what I caught earlier.

I dip the basket of the net a couple inches into the water. We both hold our breath for that last second as Dylan expertly guides the subdued beast head-first into the net.

"Got him!" my partner exclaims as he drops his baitcasting rod on the deck and grabs the net from me. "Thanks, William!"

"No problem. Giant fish, man! Nice job!" I offer, but Dylan is so excited I don't think he hears me. He reaches into the net, firmly grips the big bass by its lower lip, and pops the hook free. Then he holds it up in front of himself and just stares with his mouth hanging open. I make my way back to my position at the nose of my boat. I turn around to check on my partner and he hasn't moved yet. He has now started repeating, "No way" over and over to himself.

"That's a beast, partner," I assure him. "You're welcome to weigh it if you'd like, but I'm pretty sure that'll go better than six." I'm hoping to snap him back to consciousness, but I also don't want to ruin his moment. I know exactly how he feels. That's a great moment when you're holding a fish like that. We have great bass fishing in Wisconsin, but a fish that size is pretty rare.

Dylan blinks and shakes his head a bit as he snaps out of his trance. "Over six pounds?" he asks. "I was thinking it was at least five, but you think six?"

"Pretty sure," I tell him.

He smiles wide. "It's definitely the biggest bass I've caught during a tournament." Then he mumbles a few more "No ways" to himself and opens the passenger side livewell lid. He pauses for one last look, lowers the monster into the water, shuts the lid, then pushes it down again with all his weight, just to be safe. "Yes!" he shouts with a big fist pump. "Yes! Yes! Yes! God,

I love this sport!"

"Nice job, Dylan," I offer.

"Thanks, William! Let's do that again!" he suggests excitedly.

"I think we just might. We've got all day."

I swing the nose of the boat out wide, a bit farther from shore. I want to try to stay on the outside edge of this weed flat and fan cast across the top of it, at least for this first pass. Funny how two minutes ago I was ready to leave, and now I can just picture all the bass swimming out in front of me. The other funny thing is that I'm not feeling any jealousy that I didn't catch that big one. Instead, I'm using the information to my advantage. Any clues about the fish's behavior or location are important for forming a plan to make the most of the rest of the day. I think this new approach to tournament fishing is going to be big! I've barely started, but I feel different today. Then I pick up my buzzbait rod and pause. Should I be throwing a Senko? After all, there's nothing wrong with paying attention to what's going on around me. The bigger fish did hit a Senko. Hmmm. But the buzzbait is working too, plus I can cover a lot more ground. So far, I have no reason to change other than I like throwing a Senko. *Stay focused on what's important,* the voice in my head reminds me. Then the voice concedes, *old habits die hard.* I smile to myself and continue casting.

* * *

As we idle our way back to the launch ramp, the mood in the boat is celebratory. There has been quite a bit of high fiveing, fist bumping, and back patting today. My partner has his biggest tournament fish ever, along with two other nice ones. He is thrilled! He stuck with the same bait all day and it got him some key bites. Unfortunately, that bait fishes slowly and tediously, so it's tough to put it in front of a lot of fish. I felt guilty about moving the boat quickly, but it seemed like the fish were active so moving fast made the most sense. I even explained that to my partner, but he kept telling me he was fine. Fact is, even though he's two fish shy of his limit, there's still a decent chance that his 11 to 12 pounds may be leading on the non-boater side. Plus, he's almost certainly got big bass locked up for the whole tournament.

As for me, I just had the single best tournament day of my career. Funny to think that it's on the day that my boat is broken and my practice was for nothing. By the end, I culled out that 3-1 that started the day. If my scale is accurate, I have nearly 20 pounds total! That's a good tournament day any-where in the country, but in Wisconsin that's really something! I am fairly confident that it's going to be the biggest bag weighed in today, and I probably just secured my spot on the six-man team for next year. I have a permanent smile, as the wind eases by my face at 6.2 mph. We round the last bend and the launch comes into sight. Boats are gathering, and being loaded onto trailers. It's usually about this time that I'm going over excuses in my head, but today I can't wait for someone to ask me how I did. I'll need to remember to be cool, but honestly, I want to stand on the front deck, beat my chest, and scream "I got 'em!"

As we move past the point that Doug's partner, Ben, had recommended, I spot the two of them floating next to one of the other teams. I see Ben give the thumbs down to the other boat. Really? I think to myself with a little ashamed excitement.

"Did you just see Ben give the thumbs down?" I ask my partner.

"Sure looked like it to me," he confirms. "If *he* didn't have a good day, you might have a *huge* lead," he adds, but I had already jumped to that conclusion myself.

Then Doug spots me. He holds up his hands to his sides–palms up, elbows tucked in, as if asking "Well?"

I hold up five fingers, the universal sign among fisherman for a full limit. I'm trying to play it down but I think he picked up on my confidence.

His eyebrows raise a bit. I'm sure he wasn't expecting that considering my crippled boat. Then he holds his hands in front of him, palms facing each other, asking "How big?"

I smile and give him a thumbs up. His eyebrows go way up. Then he smiles, nods and gives me a congratulatory thumbs up in return.

I take a deep breath and try to control my smile, but it's difficult. Man, this feels great! I focus on the feeling for a second, trying to capture it in my memory bank. So, this is what a winner feels like. Actually, I don't know for sure that I've won. This is a surprisingly good fishery. It's not impossible that someone else had their best day ever, but it really doesn't matter. Of course, it would be awesome to be in the lead, but I know that I've never fished this well before and that's the best part. Even if I'm not the winner today, I'm more confident now than I've ever been that my day will come.

I ease up to the dock and Dylan jumps out to get the truck. Along the way, I've held up my five fingers several times as fellow club members have inquired. So far, I've heard mostly hard luck stories in return. Things are looking good for me.

A small crowd gathers around my boat in the parking lot as word of my exceptional day spreads quickly. Each fish I reveal is met with more and louder "Oohs" and "Ahs" from the group. It all seems surreal as I lift my fifth big fish out of my livewell, and place it into the heavy-gauge, plastic, weigh-in bag.

"Nice job, William," someone says from behind me.

"I've only seen limits like this on TV!" one of the younger guys exclaims.

"Wait 'til you see what Dylan's got," I inform them.

I ask one of the watchers to keep my bag of fish upright while I hold a second bag open for my partner's catch. He reaches deep into his side of the livewell. Sounds of thrashing and water splashing are muffled by the boat but can't be

57

denied. After a couple attempts, he smiles and reintroduces the monster to the sunlight.

"Wow!" "Beast!" "That'll be big fish!" "Looks like this was the boat to be on today!" comes the crowd's reaction. "Let me get a picture," someone requests. Dylan is more than happy to pose with his biggest tournament bass ever.

Officially, his trophy weighs in at an impressive 6-pounds, 6-ounces. The second biggest fish for the day is one of mine at 5-pounds, 2-ounces. My total weight for Day 1 of this tournament is 20-pounds, 1-ounce. I've never weighed in over 20-pounds before. In fact, my personal best limit to this point was just under 14-pounds. Twenty pounds? Twenty pounds? I can't believe it. My face is sore from smiling and my back is sore from being patted. To put things in perspective, 14-pounds, 8-ounces is second place. There are only five guys over 10 pounds today! My one day weight might actually have a chance to win this two-day tournament. Despite the odds, I've secured my spot on the team for next year. Mission accomplished.

I check the time on my iPhone and realize that I'm going to have to hustle to make it back home by 6:30 like I promised Trixie. I shake hands with my partner and we congratulate each other one more time. Then he loads his gear into his car and heads home. I'd better call and let the wife know it's going to be close, time-wise. Even with the pressure of my schedule, I'm really looking forward to this call. I want her to hear what confident, successful William sounds like. She's had to console defeated William too many times.

"Hi honey. Did you win?"

"Hi, Trixie. Yes, I did."

"Did what?" she asks. "You won? Did you win the tournament? How much did you catch? You won?" Her excitement escalates with each question.

"Yep. I mean, not really. It's a two-day tournament. I'm in the lead today, but everyone else is fishing tomorrow. But yes, I won today. Twenty pounds, one ounce," I explain.

"Twenty pounds, one ounce?" she repeats excitedly. God, this is fun I think to myself.

"Second place is over 6 pounds behind me. I might have caught enough today to win the whole thing."

"Oh my, William! That's amazing! Congratulations dear!" she practically shouts.

"Thanks, Trixie. It feels pretty good."

"So how did it happen? Tell me how you caught them," she demands.

"Gladly," I assure her, "but I need to hit the road, so we can make it to your cousin's birthday party. I'll fill you in on the details when I get home."

Then she pauses.

"Hello? Is everything okay?" I ask.

"Oh...yes. Fine," she tries to convince me.

"What is it, Trix?"

"Um, I forgot to tell you that my cousin called and it turns out she's not feeling well. She thinks it may be the flu."

"Really?" I ask.

"Yep. So the party has been canceled."

"Really?" I ask again.
"Yep. The flu. So there's really no reason for you to race home after all."

"Really?" I try one more time.

"Really, dear. You go out and wrap this thing up tomorrow. Do it like you did today and you'll set a new club record!" she encourages me.

"Are you sure that's okay? I can still come home and take you out," I offer.

"Are you kidding?" she laughs. "Please go fishing tomorrow," she practically insists.

"I guess I can probably crash on the floor in Doug and Ben's room." I pause. "Are you sure?"

"Absolutely!" she says enthusiastically. "Good luck tomorrow, William. I can't wait to see you tomorrow night."

"Alright," I concede. "You are an amazing wife."

"Oh," she groans as if rejecting my compliment. "Have fun and I'll talk to you tomorrow."

"Okay. Love you, dear. Good night."

"Love you. Good night," and she hangs up her phone.

Wow. I really hadn't thought I'd be fishing tomorrow. In my mind, my season was over. I'm excited to get one more day, but I was pretty satisfied with the idea of going out on a high note. I'll just have to fish well again tomorrow and make it a super high note.

* * *

Well, at least there isn't any lightning, I think to myself as I idle up the river for Day 2 in the pouring rain. And to be honest, it's kind of nice that I can't go 70 mph today.

The river has a dark, cold look to it. As I pull up to the island where I started yesterday, I can't really see the tips of the weeds just under the surface like

I could then. Dylan and I ended up making several trips around this island, so I'm fairly confident I know where the weed edge is, I just can't see it.

With the rain falling as hard as it is right now, I really don't feel like the buzz-bait that served me well yesterday would be a great choice. Instead, I reach for a medium-diving, square-lipped crankbait. I'll still be able to cover water and trigger reaction strikes, but this lure dives down to the fish, rather than making them come up to the surface. I can feel the bait's diving bill digging into the bottom as it scoots along. Then it hits a limb. I feel it hesitate, then climb its way up, over and bang into a second limb. But just as its about to climb over, it gets heavy and stops suddenly. I set the hook hard and the bait doesn't budge. It's locked securely in the branches below the surface. I was sure that was a fish, but with the pouring rain, it's a bit harder to discern the subtle differences. I shake my line but the bait is stuck. I hate to disturb this potential fish holding spot without covering it thoroughly, but I'll have to go get it. I ease my boat right up to the end of the tree and snap my line a few more times. Nothing. It isn't very deep here so I know I can get to the lure. I position the boat right over it and reel the tip of my rod down into the water until I feel it stop at the lure's line tie. I give a gentle push. Nothing. "Seriously, tree?" I ask out loud and push at the lure again. Then I push a little harder and shake the rod. I feel my patience growing short. "That lure costs $11, tree," I try to reason with it. I reel down to the lure from a slightly different angle and push hard and shake the rod violently until I hear and feel a sick "crack" noise. I let my neck go limp and my chin goes down to my chest in disgust. My eyes are closed and I take a deep breath. Slowly, I pull the rod out of the water to inspect, but I already know what I'm going to see. I've broken the tip of my favorite crankbait rod and snapped the line without retrieving my lure. "That was an expensive cast. Thanks, tree," I vent.

All right, I guess that's just the cost of doing business, I tell myself. *I have lots more crankbaits and my older, backup, crankbait rod. Just take a minute to retie and settle down. I've got a long day ahead of me. Keep it together.* I make a few casts and decide this will work just fine. It's not quite as sensitive as my broken rod, but it should do the job. But as I approach the next tree in the water, I find that my casting is less accurate. I'm a good two feet from the tree. To be

61

effective, a crankbait needs to bang into and bounce off of cover. I'm not sure if I should blame the new rod, or if I'm a bit scared of hanging up again and losing another expensive bait. Either way, it's unacceptable. I pick up my Senko rod and decide to work each piece of wood cover slowly and thoroughly. On the third tree, my line jumps as a hungry bass inhales my bait. I reel up the slack line and set the hook hard. The fish swims out from under the limb where he was hiding and immediately under the limb next to it. The reeling stops as I can't make any more progress. He's got me wrapped up. "Nooo," I groan as I kick the trolling motor on high to hustle over to the tree. I pull until it feels like I'm just below the line's breaking point. Nothing. Then I give him slack. Nothing. I reel the line tight again and just try to feel him. I'm not feeling any movement anymore. Quickly, I race around to the other side of the tree. I pull hard and the lure pops free, sans bass. I whip the lure back down into the water in disgust. "Perfect," I shout to no one.

I take a moment to retie and regain my focus. *Alright, plenty of time,* I tell myself. *Shake it off.*

At the next tree, my patience and focus is rewarded with a small keeper. The scale reads 2 pounds, 2 ounces. "At least I'm on the board," I try to encourage myself. Now second place needs more than nine pounds to take me. But I don't find much comfort in that thought. It occurs to me that if what I'm doing takes a dump today, maybe these conditions will help the guys who struggled yesterday. Just keep fishing, I remind myself. Worry about your fish, not your competitors.

I round the point of the island, looking forward to the backwater side where we caught our bigger fish yesterday. This is where I'll make up for lost ground. But instead of any redemption, my heart sinks as I notice another bass boat, one that I don't recognize, working the weed flat I was headed for. *Are they locals? Are they from another tournament? Why in the world would they be out here fishing in the rain, today?* my brain asks disgustedly. *Because that's just your luck!* my brain answers itself. I watch from a distance, trying to determine which way they're headed, how they're fishing and whether it's worth it to fish behind them. After a few minutes I decide, "This sucks," and I pull the trolling motor out of the water, headed for...well, actually I don't know where I'm headed.

* * *

As I make my way back to the weigh-in, my spirit isn't soaring like yesterday. I have four fish in the livewell, but my total weight is only a little more than eight pounds. I've done the math and it's still fairly possible that I've won, but the idea of victory doesn't seem nearly as sweet as it did yesterday. Today was a failure because of me. If I do squeak out a victory, it will be despite my weak performance. Once I started to derail, I just didn't have the mental toughness to get back on track today. Then I remember the books I have ordered and my training plan for the off-season. I witnessed the power of a strong mental performance yesterday.

It was as if I could do no wrong. Today feels like most tournaments I've fished in the past. I will make sure that all of my future tournaments feel like yesterday.

My total two-day weight of 30 pounds, 2 ounces was, in fact, just barely enough to give me my first tournament victory. It was close, but I got it. Receiving the trophy feels pretty good, but it feels to me like my monster Day 1 sack is almost forgotten because of my Day 2 showing. It almost makes it seem like Day 1 was a fluke. Even the blind squirrel finds a nut every once in a while. Eight pounds is more like what we expect from old Bill Buckner.

On the ride home I replay the events of the day in my head. I make note of my poor decisions and actions. I imagine myself faced with the same challenges, but in my imagination I make better choices and let myself feel what that would have been like. I make it my goal to have as many Day 1 performances as possible next year. It's going to be a good year.

I call Trixie.

"Hi, honey. Did you win?" she asks on cue.

"I *did* win, Trixie." She squeals with excitement. I continue, "I won the tournament. I won a spot on the team for next year. I won a deeper understanding of how this all works. And most of all, I won the right to tell my beautiful, tirelessly supportive wife that I won."

She didn't respond right away so I gave her a few seconds.

"Wow, you've really been thinking about this," she laughs, but I think she may also be crying.

"It's been quite a weekend," I confirm.

"Well that is great news," she tells me. "I am very happy for you and proud of you."

"Thank you," I respond sincerely.

"Dinner will be ready when you get here," she tells me. "I can't wait to see you."

"Likewise, dear. That sounds fantastic. I'll be home at about 6:30."

"Perfect. Drive safe."

"Will do," I promise.

"And, William...congratulations." The way she says it hits me hard and deep. All of a sudden I feel like I might cry.

"Thanks. See you soon," I blurt out and hang up before I get too emotional.

"Quite a weekend," I say to myself.

Ch 10
Back To Work

"Well, Mr. Buckner, she's all fixed up. The total bill came to $2,306, and it looks like your insurance is taking care of everything but the $500 deductible," the service manager tells me over the phone.

"Perfect. What time are you guys open until this evening?" I ask.

"Someone will be here until 6:00 today," he informs me.

"Great. I'll swing by after work. Thanks for getting it taken care of so quickly. You guys are the best." I know it seems like I may be piling it on a bit thick, but it never hurts to form a good working relationship with your local marina.

"Our pleasure. Thanks, William." We both hang up.

Well, $500 isn't terrible, but it's a good part of what I won at that tournament. It just sucks that it's possible to do that kind of damage while carefully and slowly loading on to my trailer at a public launch ramp. At least it would be a better story if I was running full blast across an ankle-deep mud flat filled with stumps, on my way to some secret backwater area. Honestly, I'd prefer if I had no stories that involved costly repairs, but it seems to be a part of the game.

Just then, Ian pokes his head into my office.

"Knock, knock!" he says aloud, rather than actually knocking, and then laughs as if he had just said something funny. "How'd the big tourney go?" he continues as he makes himself welcome in the chair in front of my desk. "Did we have another classic Bill Buckner performance?" More laughter.

"Actually, it was a pretty good weekend. I won the tournament," I inform him coolly and confidently.

"Really?" he asks sounding impressed. Then he thinks about it for a second.

"What, nobody showed up?" More stupid laughter.

"Actually, everybody showed up. We had 30 boats. Some of the best fishermen in this half of the state were there," I explain.

"Hmm. Well nice job, Billy Boy!"

"It's William," I correct him, but he doesn't hear me over his laughter. *What is he laughing about?* I wonder.

"So what was the biggest fish?" he asks.

"The guy in the back of my boat caught one that was nearly six and a half pounds."

Ian smiles wide. "I knew it! So, you let some rookie beat you out of the back of your boat?" He starts to laugh louder.

"Absolutely not," I insist. "I had twice as much weight as him. But you asked about big fish. My personal big fish was 5-9. Most days that would be big bass. The fact is, my smallest bass was nearly four pounds that day." I didn't shout, but it was obvious I was serious and annoyed.

Finally he stops laughing. "Aw, c'mon. I'm just playing with you," he says. "Nice job, Buckner."

"Thanks." Then I remain silent, hoping we're finished with this conversation. Normally, I would talk fishing for hours with anybody, but there's just something about this guy that I can't stand. I mean, how does saying that you're just playing give you license to say crappy things to people?

66

He rises from the chair and tries to look...I'm not sure what that look is. Dejected? Like his feelings have been hurt? Then he straightens up, like he's the bigger man.

"Nice job, Buckner," he repeats as he slips through the doorway. Then he stops and spins around. "Any white bass at all?"

"No white bass this weekend," I answer.

"We'll have to get out there sometime," he declares. "I'll show you how to catch some old white bass." Now he's laughing again.

"Sounds like a plan," I reply.

I can hear his laughter as he heads down the hall, making small talk with everyone he passes.

I'm gonna need some coffee.

Ch 11
Research

I was hoping I'd find my eBay purchase waiting for me when I got home, but no such luck. After dinner and hanging out with the girls for a bit, I excuse myself to my upstairs office, eager to start my new quest.

I decide that I'll start with some easy reading before I get into the heavy-duty, mental lifting. *Bass Wars: A story of fishing fame and fortune.* Hmm. It's from 1988. I imagine a lot of the ideas are still relevant, plus it's just old enough that some of the differences might be nostalgic and charming.

Almost immediately, the book is focusing on Rick Clunn. Not only is he the most successful and revered angler of that time, he's also described as "weird." It seems that his Zen, tree-hugging, introspective ways were well known, but not really embraced by most of his peers. "Wow, he was really into the mental stuff even 25 years ago. This is exactly what I've been thinking about. How can there not be more books on this subject? Man I can't wait to read the book series Clunn wrote!"

In a flash, two hours have passed. I am completely digging this story! The characters are exactly like me and the people I know. I totally relate to their feelings and understand the decisions they make. It's amazing how some things haven't changed a bit since this story was written. The more I read about Clunn, the more excited I get about my plan. I glance at my iPhone to check the time. I could easily stay up reading until I've finished *Bass Wars,* but I suppose my boss would not find that a suitable excuse for missing work tomorrow. Plus, I've got all winter. I find a BASS shield logo sticker in a pile of mail on my desk, slide it into the gutter between pages 98 and 99, and close the cover.

I look at my phone again. 10:05. Then I take a quick look at the weather forecast. It actually looks like it's going to be pretty nice this weekend. The tournament season is over but that doesn't mean fishing season is over. Reading this book has got me all fired up to hit the water.

I pull up my text window and type a quick message.

"Doug- Heading to the river on Saturday. Weather looks good. You in?"

I haven't fished with Doug for a while. I miss days on the water with him. I'm hoping we'll get to spend several more days out before the water freezes. Plus, I can't wait to tell him about all my new ideas and big plans. We are going to dominate next year!

"r u gonna take me to ur new hot spots? wut time u b here?" he replies. He knows I hate stupid texting shorthand. That's why he does it.

"5:30," I type back.

After a brief pause my phone buzzes. "2 early imo. but ok c u."

I laugh and type, "VFD."

Bzzz. Bzzz. "?"

"Very Funny, Dick." I press send and chuckle to myself.

Another pause, then Bzzz. Bzzz. "u mean doug?"

"Nope."

Ch 12
Destiny

It's still basically dark when we arrive at the ramp. I turn off the truck and step out. The gravel of the parking lot crunches under my shoes, breaking the perfect silence. I am headed to the boat to begin preparations for launching, but first I stop, stretch, and take a minute just to enjoy my setting. As predicted, the air is unseasonably warm and the wind is calm–nonexistent, in fact. I tip my head back and breath the sweet, musky river air while I stare at space. The western sky is alive with blinking stars, while the eastern horizon is just starting to hint of the dawning day.

"Told you 5:30 was too early," Doug jabs at me.

I don't respond. I'm still looking up.

"God, it's gorgeous out here," he tells me, pausing to take in the moment for himself.

We're really not in a hurry. I'm glad we got here early. I hate to feel rushed, especially when we're just "fun fishing."

"It should be a good day," Doug says as if he needs to convince me.

"You got that right, brother," I assure him.

* * *

Two aggressive attacks on my buzzbait without a hook-up, convince me that while they are willing to come to the surface, they aren't committing to the speedy, steady retrieve. I pick up my topwater rod rigged with a favorite, well-worn Rapala Skitter-Pop.

71

"So is this the secret spot from that tournament?" Doug asks.

"Kind of."

"Kind of?!" he recoils as if I just attacked him. "Either it is or it isn't. Don't tell me you're holding out on me!" he accuses with loads of overacted drama.

"Settle down, Hollywood. I mean 'kind of' in that we caught some fish here, but the best spot is just up ahead. Sheesh." I give Doug a playful look and pretend like I'm exhausted from talking to him. He's giving me the same look. "I'll be sure to tell you exactly when you should expect to start catching fish," I continue.

He flicks his wrist and his spinnerbait lands with a gentle splash. "*You're* Hollywood," he grumbles.

The spinnerbait is a pretty good call. We've already seen that there are active fish in the area. The thing about a spinnerbait is it works equally well zipping just above the tips of the submerged weeds or bumping into the tangled tree branches.

Doug makes a perfect little rolling, sidearm flip cast and sets his bait in a triangle-shaped opening formed by two intersecting logs and the shoreline. He begins winding and flexes the rod tip to get the blades turning. The bait catches the log farthest from shore, hesitates briefly, then rolls up and over. Textbook. A large, shadowy figure appears from under the log. Doug gasps, drawing my attention. Then we both see the white flash of belly as it grabs the spinnerbait and returns to its spot under the log.

"Big one," he tells me as he rears back to set the hook.

"Nice, Doug," I offer my encouragement as the fish thrashes on the surface. "You want some help with that one?" I ask, but without waiting for an answer, I kneel down at the edge of the boat and roll up my right sleeve. "Good fish, Dougy!" I shout. "Nice and easy!"

After a few short but powerful surges under the boat, the big bass rolls on its side at the surface and Doug leads him toward me.

"Get him! Get him! Get him!" Doug yells as my thumb locks down tightly on the fish's lower lip. I pause for a second to get my balance, then hoist the trophy over the bass boat's short gunnel.

"Yes!" Doug cries. He's half hugging me, half patting me on the back, and half using me to keep himself from collapsing. "Oh my God!" he says as we exchange my thumb for his in the beast's mouth. He holds it up in front of himself and admires his catch. "Oh my God!" he repeats. I struggle to my feet and get my first really good look.

"Oh my God!" I join him. This fish is every bit as big as the one my partner caught in that tournament, maybe a bit bigger. "Dude, that fish is pushing seven pounds," I tell him what he already knows.

"This is a beast, William." He bounces the fish lightly in front of himself as if he's weighing it with his arm. "It might go seven," he confirms.

"Lets put it in the livewell for a minute," I suggest. "We'll get the scale out and get the camera all ready. Give her a chance to rest and then we'll get a bunch of pictures."

"God, it's a beast," he tells me again, as he lowers it into the well.

Now, Doug has fished all over the country. He's even been to Mexico twice. He has caught several fish bigger than this, but I'm pretty sure this is his biggest bass from the state of Wisconsin.

"The scale is in the compartment under your left foot," I inform Doug while digging through the big storage locker up front in search of the camera.

"This is some sweet hot spot you've found here," he praises me.

73

"It does seem like it has all the right ingredients," I agree, "but give yourself some credit. That was a perfect cast, and you fought her flawlessly. Hell, I had just worked that tree ahead of you and I didn't catch her."

"Yeah, but that's you," he teases. "I think you've found a real honey hole."

"I don't know. Obviously, it's a good area for these conditions," I agree. "Maybe it'll hold up over time, but I'm still giving you the credit."

He looks at me suspiciously, then I can see his face change as he gets an idea. "Let's just call this my spot then," he says with a stupid grin.

"Fine. Doug's Island," I allow. "Let's get some measurements and some pictures and get her back in the water."

"Good idea," he agrees. He opens the livewell lid and stares in. "Oh my God!" he says with a smile. He reaches in and grabs the fish on the first try. I had forgotten how big it looked. He holds it up and I snap a picture.

"Your hat is making a big shadow across your face. Tip your hat back and I'll spin the boat around," I direct. "That's better. Now, hold it a little higher. Now, one where you're looking at the fish. Awesome! God, that thing is a beast!" I click the green button on the camera to review the pictures. "Wait 'til you see these! You're gonna freak!" I promise.

"Where's your bump board?" Doug asks. "Let's get some measurements and get her back in the water."

"Right here." I had found it when I was getting the camera.

Mouth closed. Tail pinched. Twenty-two and a half inches.

"Wow," I say.

"Wow," Doug repeats.

I zero the scale and hand it to him. He hooks it under the monster's big fat jaw and hoists it up. The fish jerks once, but then hangs still.

"Six point...no...seven...nope...six...point...nine. Wait...seven point zero?" He holds extra still and stares at the readout. "Nope. Six point nine."

"Wow," I say.

"Wow," Doug repeats.

We both take a long pause to look the beast over one last time.

"Alright, I'd better get her back," he announces and kneels at the edge of the boat.

"Back to Doug's Island," he commands the fish. He supports her just below the surface with his hand under her belly. It takes only a couple seconds before the fish lunges from his grasp and glides out of sight.

Doug rinses his hands in the river, then claps them together hard, putting an audible exclamation point on the past five minutes.

"Well that was alright," he says as he stands back up. "Thanks for the assist, bro," he tells me and offers his fist for bumping.

"Boom," I tell him.

"Boom," he repeats. Then he pauses and gives me a funny look. "So, make sure to tell me when we get to the good spot, please."

"Will do," I laugh, "but I'm telling you it had more to do with your performance than the spot."

"My performance? I'm just huckin' a spinnerbait." He raises one eyebrow. "You're not trying to get out of taking me to your best new spots are you?"

he teases, but I sense a hint of accusation in his voice.

"What? Oh, sweet tap-dancing Jesus, Doug. Yes, I'm taking the secret of the magic spot with me to the grave."

"I knew it!" he plays along.

"Actually, I've just been doing some studying lately and I think that real fishing success might not come from secret spots or secret lures."

"They sure don't hurt," he teases.

I continue without letting his comment derail me. "I'm starting to think that your mental abilities and inner voice can guide you to more fish than any secret insider information can."

Doug stops smiling and looks at me like I'm crazy. "Inner voice? You're kidding, right?"

"No, I think there's something to it. If you take the time to train and master your thoughts you can achieve some amazing results. It's been proven," I try to convince him.

"Master your thoughts?" he mocks. "Now you sound like Rick Clunn."

"Yes! Clunn!" I answer excitedly. "You've heard that Clunn is into that? You know, he attributes his success to his mental toughness."

"Yeah, success 20 years ago," Doug says dismissively.

"Hey! He's still competing!" I counter.

"Seems like he hasn't been much of a threat for a while. If he's got this mental stuff figured out, and mental power wins tournaments, why doesn't he dominate now?"

"He'd out-fish you any day," I challenge, knowing it's a weak response. Part of me wonders if Doug is making a solid point, but another part of me knows there must be a reasonable answer. Plus, if I let him totally win this argument, it will be even tougher to convince him that we need to study this stuff over the winter.

"Well, you got me there," he admits very sarcastically.

I'm regretting bringing it up. I realize now that I don't have enough of the facts to be very persuasive. I really should have studied more before trying to share it with him.

"Anyway, we should probably be casting instead of debating. The conditions are perfect right now," I try to change the subject.

Doug gives me a long look with one eyebrow raised. "Yeah, time's a-wastin'," he agrees. "I want to get me another giant!"

We fish for the next 10 minutes without a word and without a bite.

"Lets pack it up and make a little run, Doug. I've got a spot in mind down by the quarry."

"You're the guide," he responds, and gets his gear buckled down for the 15-mile run.

I stow the trolling motor and organize my rods on the front deck. Then I hop down into the drivers seat, fasten my life vest and fire up the big motor.

"Man, that fish was huge," I declare as I reach over and pat him solidly on the shoulder. Again, I'm regretting bringing up the "mind power" thing. I don't want it to spoil the day so I've decided I'll be the bigger man and try to lighten the mood–put it behind us. But to be honest, I'm really kind of pissed just beneath the surface. He should have some respect for my ideas. I'm not an idiot, plus I'm a better fisherman than he is. Alright, maybe not, but I'm as good as he is. If he wants to keep his head in the sand, I'll leave him in my dust next year. Ugh, but I don't want a teammate who's not on my level for team events. Damn it, Doug! I shouldn't have brought it up.

I idle out to the main channel marker buoy and turn downstream. A quick check port and starboard and I put the HotFoot to the floor. In an instant, the boat practically leaps out of the water and gathers speed quickly. I don't know if it's the cold fall air, or the newly re-worked prop, but this thing is running great today.

I love the fishing part of bass fishing, but I have to admit that I also love the bass boat part of bass fishing. My boat can burn across the water at speeds in the mid-60s, and it's really only middle of the pack by today's boat standards. Modern bass boats are awesome high-performance machines. The idea is that you'll spend less time getting from one spot to the next, and thus maximize your fishing time during a tournament day, but the truth is they're just a blast to drive!

We round a big left hand bend in the main river just as the sun peaks over the treeline ahead of us. Amazing rays of burning gold streak across feathery, purple clouds.

I lean over to Doug and yell to be heard over the outboard and rushing wind noise. "Wow, check that out Dougy!"

He nods his approval.

"Good stuff, man," I continue. "Good day!" But when I glance at him again, I notice his face has changed. He looks a little concerned.

He leans over to me and shouts, "I thought we were going to have the river to ourselves this morning." He points at the other shoreline. "Bass boat."

I follow his gaze and spot the intruder. He's still a good ways up ahead and well off the main channel, but I recognize immediately that something isn't right.

"He's in an odd spot," I yell.

"Do you recognize who it is?" he responds.

I fix my eyes and squint. As we draw closer, more details come into focus. It's a dark-colored boat. A Ranger, maybe? And it looks like the outboard is trimmed all the way up. Actually, it looks like the cowling is removed. That's never good.

Doug is coming to the same conclusions as we get closer and closer. "We'd better check it out," he calls.

I've already started to slow down. The driver of the other boat realizes that we've spotted him and begins waving his arms over his head to alert us that he needs assistance.

I set our boat down off of pad a couple hundred yards away and turn out of the main channel toward the distressed boat.

"Seavers," Doug says without emotion.

"Cam?" I ask.

"Cam," he confirms. His tone of voice sounds like he would just as soon leave him there.

"What have you got against him?" I inquire.

"He's a know-it-all, and frankly, I just don't trust him. He seems a little greasy." Doug's normally playful voice is cold.

As we get closer Cam calls out, "Man, am I glad to see you guys!"

We idle the last 30 yards and finally pull up alongside him.

"You alright?" I ask. Doug leans out of our boat and grabs onto the edge of Cam's just before they bump together.

"Yeah, I'm fine, thanks, but this piece of crap motor has seen better days," he complains, then gives the cowling on his back deck a half-hearted kick.

"That's new, isn't it? What's it doing?" I ask.

He holds up three fingers. "Third season. Not sure exactly what's wrong, but it's probably not good. I was running up the main channel when it sputtered once, made a loud, metallic bang, then stopped cold."

"That sucks!" I offer.

"Yeah, not awesome. I'll have to check, but I'll bet the warranty just ran out. We'll see. What sucks most at the moment is being stuck. And of course, this is the stretch of river where my cell doesn't get any reception." He pulls the phone out of his front pocket to confirm his own statement. He holds it overhead and squints at the display. "Yep. No service." He shakes his head with disgust.

"Well, we can give you a tow," I suggest, happy to do a local fishing legend a favor.

"Where did you put in?" I ask.

"All the way up at the launch behind the high school." He cringes a little as he says it, knowing that it's a long way and a big favor he's asking.

"Well then we'd better get started," I reply cheerily. "I've got a good tow rope in the far back compartment." I know it's going to eat into our fishing day, but I've been trying to figure a way to Cam's good side for years. This may work out well for everyone.

"What about the launch right there at the park?" Doug chimes in and points to a small ramp on the opposite shore. His voice sounds odd since it's the first thing he has said since we pulled up to Cam. After a moment of awkward silence while we all consider this new voice's suggestion, I say, "But his truck is up at the high school." Cam remains silent.

"Right," Doug says impatiently, rolling his eyes at me a little bit. "But we could pull his boat to the launch right there," he points at it again, "then all ride in your boat at full speed, up to his truck, and he can drive here and get his boat."

We all look at each other for another awkward moment.

"I guess that would work," I agree. "Either way, I guess. Cam, what do you want to do?" He hadn't weighed in yet.

"I guess that would work," he says kind of dejected. "I guess I could drive back down here. Whatever you guys want to do."

"Perfect. Then it's decided. Let's get this broken boat over to the park," Doug says, clearly trying to end this discussion.

I look to Cam for his reaction. Doug's probably right, but I'm more concerned with forming a bond with my new friend.

"Sure," Cam says, trying to sound grateful. "I appreciate the help."
We exchange weak smiles and I hand him one end of the tow rope.

* * *

Using the trolling motor for the last few feet of his broken boat's journey, he pulls the nose up onto the sandy shore near the launch. He uses his anchor rope to secure the craft to a nearby tree. After stowing all his gear and locking all the compartments, he meets us at the end of the pier. With Cam seated between Doug and I, we start idling out to the main channel.

"That's a shame," Cam laments as he looks to the sky, checking weather conditions. "I had a feeling they were really going to bite today."

"No kidding. Doug got his personal best earlier this morning," I blurt out. Doug shoots me a hard look, and I quickly realize that I may have betrayed his trust. But still, I want Cam to know that I can get on some good fish. Why not? It was my spot anyway.

Cam notices Doug glaring at me and laughs a bit. "Relax, partner. It's not a tournament day," he teases. Doug backs down slightly, but he still doesn't smile. "Congrats, Doug," he offers.

"A seven pounder," I add excitedly.

"Six-nine," Doug corrects. "And, personal best only for this state," he clarifies.

"Nice fish. Big bass for the river," Cam assures him.

Rather than saying thanks, Doug grunts and nods. Actually, he may have said thanks, but it was definitely not a polite thanks.

After a good 10 seconds of uncomfortable silence Cam asks, "Crankbait?"

"Nope," Doug replies.

After a couple more seconds of awkwardness, I answer, "Spinnerbait." Doug shoots me the look again, but I don't care. He's being a baby. He's just proving that he's not approaching this on the same level I am. I wonder how Cam would feel about my new fishing philosophy?

"Yep, spinnerbait," I continue. "But, for my money, I don't think the specific bait or color are really the reason you catch fish most of the time."

Doug glares at me and rolls his eyes.

"I totally agree," Cam chimes in.

Doug rolls his eyes back the other direction so hard I think I heard them rolling.

Cam continues, "Don't get me wrong. I think you need to make an intelligent lure choice based on current conditions, but confidence can be just as important."

"Exactly!" I exclaim. "Thank you!" Now I shoot Doug my own triumphant look.

"Confidence?" Doug mumbles mockingly. "I'm confident you guys are both way too far up in your own heads."

"Seriously?" Cam asks in a tone of voice that reminds us all that he is by far the most successful angler of the three of us.

Doug seems to pick up on the signal and takes his tone down a notch. "Look, I'm saying that maybe the big shot pros focus on their mental games, but I don't think it's going to make that much difference to some weekend wannabes like us."

"But if we ever want to get to that level, shouldn't we be trying to learn some of those more subtle, advanced techniques?" I try to reason with him. I really feel like I need my tournament partner to at least acknowledge that he would consider it.

Doug doesn't respond.

"Absolutely," Cam confirms.

Doug still doesn't respond.

I pass the green buoy that marks the main channel, indicating we're safe to run. I turn the wheel clockwise, as I check upstream and downstream.

"You guys ready?"

Doug nods.

Cam isn't done with our discussion. He gives it one last try. "I just figure if it's good enough for Rick Clunn, it's good enough for me."

My face lights up as I give Doug a goofy, raised eyebrow smile. I believe his eyes might roll right out of his head.

"I couldn't agree more!" I tell Cam enthusiastically.

Slowly we idle upstream in the main channel. I'm waiting to see if Doug has any more closed-minded, non-tournament-winning thoughts he wants to share, while hoping Cam wants to continue to prove we should be fishing together. We move in silence until I'm sure the conversation is over. A quick check over each shoulder and the big outboard roars to life as I push the accelerator to the floor.

* * *

Obviously, I refused Cam's offer to pay me for my time and gas. However, I did agree to let him buy me a beer at Molly's Tap sometime and exchanged contact info with him.

He honks the horn and waves as he pulls his truck and empty trailer out of the parking lot and onto the highway. Doug and I sit in my boat at the end of the pier, watching and making sure Cam gets going okay. Well, actually, I'm making sure he's okay. Doug is only here because I'm driving the boat.

Without a word, I turn the key and the big motor rumbles to life. The lower unit gears clunk into action and we begin idling back toward the main river.

The sun is well above the trees, but we've still got all day to fish. I'm trying to remain optimistic, but I get the feeling that Doug is going to be less than pleasant to share a 19-foot platform with for the next eight hours. I wonder how many big fish we're going to have to catch before he'll be willing to have a mature, open-minded discussion about advanced fishing philosophies? I wish I knew more about the subject myself. I'll bet Cam knows a ton about it. I wonder how much he'd be willing to tell me? I look at Doug. He's just staring ahead silently. It sure would be easier if I could get him on my side before next season. I wonder how Trixie would react if I told her I was dumping her brother. I doubt she'll be impressed if I tell her that Cam has won a bunch of tournaments over the years.

"So, you got any spots in mind?" I ask as we enter the main channel.

"You're the guide," he responds coldly with just a hint of sarcasm.

"You're the guy who caught his personal best today," I remind him.

He stares forward in silence. I turn my head to look at him and wait for a response.

"C'mon. Don't you have any ideas about where we should fish?" I ask.

"I guess I just don't have the mental capacity of you and Cam," he pouts.

"Aw, Jesus Christ, Doug! Just because I wanted to take an opportunity to learn from someone who's fishing on a different level than myself, you're offended?"

He looks at me but doesn't answer right away. Finally he speaks. "Different level?"

"Yes, different level. You know he's kicked our asses dozens of times. Maybe if we start thinking like him, we'd have a chance."

Doug shakes his head, not in disgust, but rather in pity. "You know the first thing Cam asked was what lure I was using."

Ch 13
Help Yourself

Most years I would be going through withdrawals, having winterized the boat two weeks ago. But new books and videos have been arriving at my door almost daily, stealing my focus. This winter I have a mission that will occupy all the free time I have.

I've started the past five mornings with meditation and exercise. Last night I tried a visualization program. In addition to my coffee trick at work, I've been utilizing a breathing regimen that really does seem to calm me and help me make better decisions. For now, I'm just trying everything. Eventually, I'll develop a program that is custom-suited for my tournament fishing goals. Goals! That reminds me, I need to set my goals. I'm not talking about wishful New Year's resolutions. I've learned that there are very specific ways to determine effective goals. Even the words that I choose to define them can determine whether I'll keep them or not.

Meditation seems to come up in everything I read. I'm struggling with the whole concept a bit, but I guess it makes some sense from a logical standpoint. From what I've learned, there's actually a ton of scientific data and research that backs it up. The tough part for me is knowing if I'm doing it right. How can I measure the results? If I were trying to grow bigger shoulders I could count and record the number of reps I perform. I could watch my form in a mirror. I would know that this week I'm able to lift more weight than I did last week, and I would see the results. My shirts would fit differently. I could prove my success with a simple tape measure. Measuring the success of a meditation program is more abstract. I suppose, just like using a muscle causes it to grow and get stronger, repeatedly flexing my brain's ability to focus is the way to strengthen that ability.

Meditation works very nicely in conjunction with a visualization program. Visualization is an interesting concept, and if done properly, the brain can't tell the difference between an experience that is imagined and one that actually happened. Would someone who fishes year-round be more comfortable and "in tune" than someone who only spends six months in a boat? Also, my virtual experiences can be 100 percent positive. If for the six months of winter I never lose a big fish, I'll be far more relaxed and confident when reeling one in during a tournament.

And in my *spare*, spare time I've been chipping away at an incredibly eye-opening book called *Knowing Bass* by Dr. Keith Jones. Jones is an actual scientist. I'm only a couple chapters in, but I am blown away. The information he presents about bass behavior is based on unbiased, accurate, scientific studies. When thought about logically, it makes perfect sense. It is human nature to extend our view and understanding of the world to all other creatures. We assign human attributes to bass because that is the simplest way for us to explain and communicate concepts. The fact is a bass can't possibly have the same perception of the world as we do because they are biologically different. I've got a lot to think about the next time I'm choosing a lure, and the programmer/analyst in me really likes the fact that I'll be able to base my decisions on logic and facts.

Oh, and I finished that *Bass Wars* book a couple days after I started it. Even though the story follows several pros of the time, Clunn is featured throughout and even gets the last word in the whole book. It really does a great job of showing the highs and lows behind the scenes of competitive fishing. Some things really haven't changed much since it was written. It scared me a bit to see myself so clearly in the guys who were willing to risk it all for the sport. I know that if I was in their shoes I would have made the same decisions. I enjoyed the book so much that I started to tell Trixie about it, but quickly realized she might not appreciate the character's blind obsession the same way I did.

For right now, I'm trying to expose myself to as many ideas and philosophies as quickly as possible so I can pick and choose the best combination. Then I'll have several months to put this plan into action. I'd like to say I know in my heart that this new course is going to have a huge impact on my whole life, but even better than that, I can feel it in the logical part of my brain! Now if I can only...

Bzzz. Bzzz. My iPhone vibrates with a text from Cam. "Hey! What's up?" I read on the display.

"Studying. Planning for next year. What's up with you?" I send. We've communicated a couple times since that day on the river. Last weekend he mentioned that his team partner for next year was looking iffy. I didn't jump on it like I should have. I left the opportunity floating there. I didn't say I wanted to fish with him, but I also didn't say I wouldn't. I'm still trying to work things out with Doug. Actually, I'm not really trying all that hard. I'm torn.

Bzzz. Bzzz. "I'm at Gander Mountain. Chronarch reels 50 percent off. How many you want?"

"Seriously? Shimano stuff never goes on sale! Are you sure?" I send.

Bzzz. Bzzz. "This opportunity will not last. How many you want?"

Well, now what does that mean? What kind of sale is this? I love Chronarchs, but I did tell myself I wasn't going to stock up for next year until after I had done all of my new studying.

Bzzz. Bzzz. "Tick tock."

Ugh. I guess I'll always need reels no matter what I learn about mental performance.

"2 please. Right-handed."

Bzzz. Bzzz. "Done. Talk to you later."

Hmm. Cool. I love Chronarchs! Half price? How does that happen? I don't think I can recall ever seeing Shimano reels on sale. Maybe they're not dominating the market like they used to. Well, in any case, that was awfully nice of my new buddy to think of me.

Ch 14
Coal In My Stocking

"Is there something wrong? You don't seem like yourself," Trixie observes from the passenger seat as we travel down the highway.

"What? No. I'm fine," I try to assure her. Actually, I am a little bit anxious about seeing her brother. I haven't seen Doug since that day we helped Cam with his boat. It's not like I've been avoiding him. I'm pretty sure I commented on a photo he posted on Facebook a couple weeks ago. I think the truth is I've already fired him as my tournament partner, at least in my mind. I just haven't figured out how to say it to him. Alright, I guess I have been avoiding him.

"I know you don't like getting together for Christmas today, because Christmas isn't actually until next weekend, but this is the only date that works for my family," she tries to reason with me.

"What? No. Everything is fine." I guess I'd prefer to celebrate Christmas on Christmas, but I really don't mind. Oh, but wait a second. At least this way, Trixie doesn't suspect that my issue is with her brother. Perfect.

"Hmmm," she says suspiciously.

"How many of my cousins will be there today?" Dacey asks from the back seat.

"All of them from Mommy's side of the family, sweetheart. Um, three," I answer, eager to get Trixie on to a new subject.

"Oh good!" she exclaims. Then in typical kid fashion asks, "How long until we're there?"

Trixie chuckles, then answers, "Dace, you know we just left home five minutes ago." She points out the window. "Look. There's our Wal-Mart right there."

Dacey looks but doesn't seem satisfied with that answer. "So, how long?"

"It's a little over an hour to Grandma's house, honey," I try to help. I catch Dacey's eye in the rear view mirror. She scrunches up her cute little nose in frustration.

"Will you please just tell me when we're almost there?" she asks very seriously.

"Of course, dear. You'll be the first to know." Kids are funny. What's she going to do when I tell her we're almost there? I often wonder what she's thinking and how her young mind processes information. I really love being a dad. She's such a great kid.

Trixie's eyes are fixed on me with one eyebrow raised. She's caught me lost in my thoughts and smiling to myself like a big goof. I reach over, put my hand on top of her hand, and aim my smile at her. I know the main reason our kid is so great is because of Trixie's influence. It has occurred to me lately, she really is a pretty great wife and mother.

* * *

"Have you seen that new Rapala topwater bait–the twin prop model?" I ask Doug. It never takes long for our conversations to turn to fishing.

"Seen them?" he asks as if he's surprised. "I have two of every color!"

"I should have known," I laugh. "That's a sweet looking lure."

"I know. I'm picturing that thing sputtering across that flat behind Doug's Island during post-spawn."

"Perfect," I agree.

"Perfect is right! They're gonna kill it!" he says while pantomiming the lure with one hand and a hungry bass overtaking it from below with his other hand.

"They look every bit as good as lures costing three times as much."

"They really do," he confirms. "If you ever came by anymore I'd let you play with them," he smiles.

"Yeah, I've just been really busy lately. I'll have to do that," I half-promise. I really have been missing our time fishing together or just hanging out in his garage, talking and daydreaming about fishing. Then in an effort to get away from the momentary awkwardness, I try to get the focus back on the lures. "I'm planning to pick up a couple of those baits for myself."

"I'm glad to hear you say that. I thought you didn't care about lures anymore," Doug teases.

I look at him with one eyebrow raised, not getting the joke.

"You know? It's not about the lure? It's all about the mind?"

"Ah, of course," I confirm. "I don't suppose you've given it any more thought, have you?" I hope he says he has, but I already know the answer. I've been trying to give him some time for it to sink in. Actually, I've just been avoiding what I know is inevitable. I'm hoping to think of a way we can still remain best friends while I advance in my fishing career without him. I can't see a way. Secretly, I've been hoping that something would cause him to give up fishing altogether, so I wouldn't have to fire him.

"I have thought about it," he surprises me.

"Really?" I perk up.

"Yea, but I still think it doesn't really apply to me."

The smile falls from my face.

"Look, I don't think you shouldn't check it out if you think it will help you. I'm just saying that it doesn't suit me. I really enjoy my fishing the way I do it right now."

I nod, but don't say anything.

He continues. "I hope it does wonders for you. I really do. Why wouldn't I want my partner to catch as many fish as possible?" He smiles at me, pausing to make sure I understand.

I nod again.

"That reminds me, we need to get signed up for next year's Big River series. I got an e-mail from them last week. Did you get that?" he asks.

"Hmm. Nope, I don't think so," I lie. "I'll have to see how my vacation hours line up with their schedule," I continue to lie.

Doug looks at me suspiciously. He's right to be suspicious. What does that even mean, vacations hours lined up with their schedule? I know I need to tell him the truth, but not here at the family Christmas party. I convince myself I don't want to ruin Christmas.

I try to clarify. "What I mean is, I'm not sure how many team tournaments I'll be able to do next year. I'm really going to focus on the pro-am series."

Doug looks disappointed but not angry. This plan sounds believable, as it is somewhat true. I am going to focus on the pro-am series, but I definitely want to do some team tournaments with Cam.

"I figured you would probably want to do more pro-ams too," I try to build on my story.

"Hmm. I guess I might." He rubs his bearded chin in a thoughtful sort of way. "I hadn't really planned on it, but I think you might have a good idea there."

"Daddy!" Dacey runs into the office where Doug and I have been chatting, away from the chaos of a family gathering. Two of her cousins have followed her, but they remain just outside the door in the hallway. "Daddy, it's time to eat. Mommy said to come and get you."

"Okay, sweetheart. Thank you. We'll be there in a minute," I promise. Satisfied that she has completed her mission, she turns and runs out the door where her cousins giggle and chase after her.

I turn my attention back to Doug. "Look, let's just wait and see how things..."

"That's alright," he assures me with a smile. "Let's go eat."

Ch 15
Getting To Know You

I unzip my heavy winter coat and stomp my boots to shake the snow free as I walk through the front door of the Pinewood Diner. Cam is seated in a booth by the big front window, just as we planned. He lowers his coffee cup and waves me over.

"Hey, Buck! You want some coffee?" Without waiting for my response he motions to the waitress, but she's already on her way with a steaming pot.

Did he just call me Buck? I ask myself. *Hmm. Buck. Not a bad nickname. I can live with Buck.* "Hey, buddy," I respond. "You haven't been waiting long, have you?" I ask as I throw my coat into the booth and slide in.

"Nope, just got here. Eight, o' clock." He checks his watch. "Right on time."

I smile and raise the mug to my lips, but I can tell it's way too hot for me. I take a big soothing breath of the rich steam. "Thanks for the invite, Cam. I'm really looking forward to catching a couple through the ice. Hard to believe this is going to be my first time out this winter."

"Yeah, you are overdue," he agrees. "Nothing better than battling a couple big crappies on 2-pound-test to get you through a long, bass-free, Wisconsin winter."

I smile and nod politely. "Hey, any update on your outboard?" I inquire.

"Ugh," he responds as if this subject has really been wearing him out.

"Is it serious?" I ask with genuine concern. Of course, if you've owned and operated a bass boat for any length of time you'll have your share of hard-luck stories and really feel what the other guy is going through.

"Oh, it's serious," he confirms. "A piston seized up and the connecting rod snapped."

I wince to show I understand how serious that is.

He continues, "A piece of the rod punched a hole in the cylinder wall and another piece put a huge gouge in the crankshaft." I can see the pain on his face.

"Bad times," I console. He nods wearily. "I would imagine your insurance should take care of it though, right?"

He looks down. "Not sure. We'll see how it goes."

Well I would sure think that they should..."

"Yep. We'll see how it goes," he cuts me off. I guess he's frustrated and I don't want to make him feel worse. I decide quickly to let it go.

There's an obvious awkward pause. Cam smiles sheepishly in an attempt to reassure me. "No worries, Bill. I've got a couple ideas. I'm sure I'll get it taken care of one way or another."

I return the smile.

"Mmm, that reminds me," he declares, and produces a bag from the bench seat next to him. "This oughta get you jonesing for some bass fishing."

Oooh, I'll bet that's my Chronarchs, I think to myself as I accept the bag from him. I smile wide and set one of the two, reel-sized boxes on the table between us. My joy fades quickly as I read the package. "Citica?" I ask with disappointment and confusion. "I thought you said Chronarch?" I don't understand. I know for a fact that Cam knows the difference between the entry-level Citica and the pro-grade Chronarch. I mean, Citica's are okay, but...

"Have you guys had a chance to look at the menu?" asks a pretty 20-something, with her hair held up behind her head with one of those big clamp things and a white, coffee-stained apron tied neatly around her thin waist.

"Oh! Um, let me see. I guess I'll have..."

"Look dear," Cam interrupts, "we're going to need a minute. I'll let you know when we're ready."

Her pleasant smile disappears. "O...kay," she says with a bit of attitude and turns to leave. I'm pretty sure I caught her eyes rolling after she thought she had turned far enough that we wouldn't see. Maybe I just imagined it, but I don't think so.

"So open it," Cam goes right back to our conversation as if nothing had happened. He's pointing with his eyes at the Citica box on the table between us.

"Look, I don't want to seem ungrateful, but I thought..."

"Open it," he insists.

I pull the top flap and expose the reel. "Wait, what's this? A Chronarch?" I look to Cam for an explanation. "Both of them?" I ask.

"You asked for two Chronarchs, didn't you?" he says confidently.

"Well, yea. But why are the boxes..."

"Two Chronarchs," he repeats.

I'm confused. *Why would Gander Mountain not have the proper packaging? Are these demo models? Where are the Chronarch boxes?* I spin the reel's handle and watch the spool whir smoothly. *This reel looks brand new. I get the impression Cam isn't going to answer any of these questions for me.*

"That's a beauty, huh?" he asks me excitedly.

"Absolutely," I agree enthusiastically. "I've always loved Chronarchs." I hesitate and try to smile at Cam. He's beaming at me from across the table, just waiting for my thanks and praise. "Why does the box say..."

"Half price," he announces proudly. "You're not gonna beat that deal."

"That's a great deal," I agree less confidently.

"And you can just pay me whenever. You know, whenever you've got the cash available." He raises his mug, takes a long, loud sip, then smiles at me like he's taken care of everything.

I close the lid on the mysterious box and place the reel back into the bag with its twin. I make eye contact with Cam. He's clearly waiting for me to thank him.

"Yeah, that's great. Thanks, man. I'll get you the cash next time we get together."

"Like I said," he gives me a cheesy wink, "whenever."

* * *

"Holy moly, that's a big crappie!" Cam exclaims as I hold the speckled fish out in front of myself to get a good look.

"What do you think?" I squint trying to size it up. "13 and a half? 14?"

"It might go 14," he confirms.

100

I dig into my coat pocket with my free hand and locate my iPhone. "Here. Get a couple pictures for me, would ya?" I ask.

Reluctantly, he takes the camera. "You're not planning to post these pictures on Facebook or something are you?"

"Facebook? Oh, maybe. I guess so," I admit, feeling guilty but not sure why. His face sours. "I would just prefer to keep my spot a secret."

"Oh," I manage to respond. *Is he serious?* I wonder to myself.

Before I can ask a follow-up question, he forms a plan. "Here. I'll just shoot from an angle where you can't see any landmarks in the background." Then he rises from his overturned bucket seat and walks across the ice to my other side. "Much better," he compliments himself. "Now, hold that piggy up...and smile...got it...now, one more...good." He tips the screen down in front of himself and confirms his work. "Looks good. Nice fish!" he tells me as he hands my phone back with a smile.

"Thanks, Cam," I say with a bit of relief. I'd hate to upset him when things have been going so well. I didn't realize that he is one of those "secret" fishermen. It's not really my style, but I guess I don't mind respecting his "secret spots." It's really...interesting, I guess... getting to know someone new. Cam definitely thinks about things differently than Doug or myself. Maybe that's the reason he's so much more successful than we are as tournament anglers.

"It's just that if you could see that old, blue house right there behind you in the picture, we'd have a crowd here next weekend," Cam informs me.

"Mmm," I acknowledge, nodding my head once. It seems unlikely to me that there would be a crowd, but I don't think there's any harm in agreeing.

"I've just been burned too many times," he continues. "I even had to break ties with my tournament partner this past fall."

"What? Wait! You mean Denny? Denny Henson? I know you said he might not fish with you next year. What do you mean you broke ties?" I realize I'm starting to ramble and don't want to seem excited, but this is amazing news! I try not to smile and wait for him to clarify.

"You know...broke ties. I'm not going to be able to fish with him anymore." I'm still trying not to smile. "Really? What happened?" The truth is I don't care what happened.

Cam looks fairly serious. His eyes lock onto mine. He hesitates briefly while trying to find the right words. "I guess I just couldn't trust that he'd keep his mouth shut, you know?"

"I know what you mean," I assure him. I don't really know exactly what he means, but if he had just told me that he needs a partner who is willing to wear a tutu and learn to speak Swahili, I would have said I know what you mean. I wonder if he's considering me as a tournament partner candidate?

Satisfied that he had answered my questions, Cam situates himself back on his bucket, opens the bail of his tiny spinning reel, and watches his tiny jig and "maggie" disappear through the hole in the ice in front of him. He turns his electronic flasher unit toward himself with the side of his foot.

I turn my attention to my own flasher. Ice fishing for panfish with an electronic flasher depth finder reminds me of playing a video game. A thick solid bar of color indicates the bottom of the lake at 24 feet. Thinner, less-dense lines from 24 feet, up to about 21 feet deep are the unit's way of representing the aquatic plants these panfish call home. At the 20-foot mark is a single line that represents my jig. If I reel in, I can watch the line move up–19 feet, 18 feet, 17 feet. Without warning, one of the lines that was pretending to be a weed, closes in on my jig line. I know that when the two lines meet I'll likely feel a slight tug on my 2-pound-test line threaded through an ultra-sensitive spring bobber on the end of my tiny spinning rod. It's definitely not like a hungry bass busting my slop frog through a thick pad canopy, but it's kind of cool in the meantime. The little line has stopped its ascent at about the 18-foot mark. I jiggle the miniature spinning rod very gently, trying to entice a strike. Then I let my lure free-fall back down 6 inches or so and continue jiggling. The "fish" line remains stationary. That's not a bad sign. At least he's still there looking at it. I reel the lure up about a foot, and the fish moves up with it. *Oh, he is getting ready,* I tell myself. Suddenly, two more "fish" lines show up just under the original line.

"Looks like we might have a school coming in," I inform my new fishing buddy.

"Yep. I've had a couple looking at my lure for the last couple...there he is!" Cam raises the tiny rod and it doubles over, pointed at the hole. "Got him!" he declares.

"Nice, Cam!" I encourage him. Then I notice the bend in my own rod. "Ooh! Me too!" I set the hook and start reeling. "Feels like another good one," I inform Cam.

"Yeah, mine too," he tells me excitedly.

Soon we both hoist above-average-sized crappies out of the frozen lake.

"That's more like it," Cam says laughing and smiling.

"Very nice," I declare.

"Better get back in there," he says, as if I might not be planning to keep fishing. "Looks like we got a school."

Over the next half-hour we both limit out on the sporty, delicious panfish, each catching a couple real beauties in the process. We both begin to organize our gear and get ready to leave the frozen lake.

"Hey, thanks again, Cam, for the invite. That was some fine fishing!"

"No problem. It doesn't compare to open water bass fishing, but it's a pretty fun way to spend a winter day," he tells me with a smile.

"Yeah, I'm dying for open water!" I inform him, hoping to continue the bass fishing talk.

"We should do some bass fishing next summer," he offers.

"Absolutely!" I agree a bit too vehemently.

He chuckles at my enthusiasm. "You and Doug doing the Spring Open up at Wabasha?" he asks matter-of-factly.

"Umm. No, I don't think Doug's going to be fishing many partner tournaments." It's not really a lie, I convince myself.

Cam tips his head to one side and raises an eyebrow. "Really?"

"Yep," I nod.

"Hmm. Maybe we should consider teaming up," he offers what I've been working on for the last three months.

I nod slowly as though I'm considering this idea for the first time. "Hmm. Maybe we should," I reason aloud.

"If we play it right, I really think we could put a hurtin' on those boys," he tells me as if I need convincing.

"I like the sound of that," I tell him. I nod again, and thrust my hand out in front of me. "Put her there, partner."

A wide smile comes over his face. He shakes my hand solidly. "Partner," he repeats.

Ch 16
Learning To Breathe

One. Two. Three. Four.

One. Two. Three. Four. Five. Six.

One. Two. Three. Four.

One. Two. Three. Four. Five. Six.

I focus on each breath.

Breathe in. One. Two. Three. Four.

Breathe out. One. Two. Three. Four. Five. Six.

My breath is the only thing on my mind at this moment. My eyes are closed but I'm very awake. It's amazing how the simple act of focusing on each breath can so dramatically calm me and improve my overall feeling.

The door to my office is closed but I can hear the little footsteps of Dacey as she races down the hall. I imagine she's headed to her room to get her PJs on. It's about that time of the evening. She told me earlier that she changed her favorite color from purple to green. Furthermore, she is going to declare a new color every year on her birthday because there are too many beautiful colors in this world to have just one favorite. She's incredibly bright and introspective for a kid her age.

Breathing! Focus on my breathing!

One. Two. Three. Four.

One. Two. Three. Four. Five. Six.

It's alright that my mind wandered for a minute. That really is what the whole exercise of meditation is about. Just like doing reps while weight lifting, I'm sharpening my ability to stay focused and strengthening my power to control my thoughts. Sure sounds like a skill that would come in handy during a tournament day.

Breathe in.

Breathe out.

Now, starting with my feet I just want to focus on how they feel. Is there any tension? Are they cold? With all of my attention focused on how they feel, I relax them fully, letting all of the tension melt away.

Next, I move to my legs. Same thing–what do I feel in my legs? Are they tired? I feel the elastic of my right sock pulled snug around my calf while my left sock has fallen to just above my ankle. Good! Now relax my legs.

Now my hips, then my stomach, my chest, shoulders, etc. Soon I am fully aware of my feelings and fully relaxed. It's pretty amazing how this simple exercise makes me feel. I'm calm. I'm grounded. I feel like I'm in tune with the world. And unlike most of the time when I take it for granted, I am very aware that I'm alive.

While this is a perfectly satisfying meditation experience, I love to use this state to my advantage and get some tournament practice in.

I picture myself in my boat racing down the river at full speed. In the blue light of early morning I can see the white rooster tails of my competitors ahead of me. The air is cool and fresh on my face. The wind rushes by my ears, drowning out nearly everything but the growl of the outboard. I can see my non-boater partner in the passenger seat, but I don't recognize his face. I know that he will not interfere with any of my plans. I know that we'll work great together and both catch a lot of fish. I feel great! I'm calm and confident. This is my day!

I begin to slow the boat as I steer toward a perfect little backwater area. The wind noise is replaced by the sounds of frogs and birds calling out to the new day. I can smell the green plants on the shore. I shut the big motor off, unzip my vest and make my way to the front deck. I take a moment to observe my surroundings. The left side of the bay seems to have a deeper cut to it where most of the current from the main river flows through. Plus, there's a small feeder creek flowing in on that side. The downstream point has several fallen trees piled up on it, forming an eddy just behind them.

I know there's a beast right on the edge of the eddy. I just know it. He's resting right in the V formed by those two tree trunks. From the rods I have out on my front deck I select a beautiful, medium-action, six-and-a-half-footer rigged with a classic perch-colored Pop-R. The rig feels perfectly balanced in my hand. I take a deep breath, lock in on the exact spot I want my cast to land, click the release button under my thumb and send my lure out on its mission. My cast lands exactly as planned, just a few feet upstream of the spot. I hesitate for two seconds while the current moves the floating bait into position. I know this will work. I reel the slack from my line and jerk the rod tip down, causing the popper to chug and gurgle as it surges forward across the water. I pause for half a second and twitch the rod tip again. Without an audible splash, the lure disappears and my line starts to move away from me. I set the hook hard, but off to the side to get the fish headed away from the tangled logjam. I feel the powerful head shake of an oversized bass telegraphed through the rod and into my hands. The fish is strong but I know I will win. He makes a run to the right, but I counter him to the left. He heads to the surface trying to shake the hook, but I change his course by jamming the fishing rod down into the water. I am in charge. I drop to one knee and reach over the gunnel. I feel the sandpaper lower lip as my thumb clamps down on my prize. The fish is actually hard to lift without rebalancing myself and getting the proper leverage. This is the biggest largemouth I've ever caught in a tournament. Heck, it's the biggest largemouth I've ever caught. As I hold the monster up in front of myself, I can feel the surge of adrenaline. My co-angler congratulates me enthusiastically. With a great deal of pride and an overwhelming sense of accomplishment, I open the livewell lid and lower the beast in. I take the time to stare at the beautiful fish. At first he's curled up, but soon finds the right angle to stretch out in the tank. I'm thrilled but I'm not surprised. I will win the tournament today, so of course I will be catching big fish.

And now, just because I can, I make the same cast again and catch another fish just as big. I'm careful to note exactly how it feels to catch fish like this. What does the air feel like? How does the river smell? How do the birds and the barges and my livewell pump sound?

At the end of the day, when the livewell can't hold any more fish, we head for weigh-in. I continue to notice how everything feels. Water soaks through the right sleeve of my tournament jersey as I wrestle my catch from the well to the weigh bag. I hear the comments coming from the boats on either side of me. My chest swells with pride as I cue up in the scale line and lift the bulging bag into the holding tank. I'm not cocky or arrogant, I'm confident. I know that I will win today. I hear the tournament director call my name as I climb the stairs to the stage. I'm the last to weigh in, so everyone knows immediately that I've won. I feel the excitement, the accomplishment. I feel the satisfaction that all of my hard work has paid off. I accept the congratulations graciously. I struggle to hold the two largest squirming fish for a picture. I feel the weight of the trophy. I notice the smooth, wooden base in one hand and the rough, cast metal of a leaping bass statue in the other hand. I can see my name etched into a plate on the base of the trophy. I am grateful and I am satisfied.

I take another deep, slow breath and open my eyes. I jump a bit to find Dacey standing right in front of me. She's wearing her pajamas and a concerned look.

"Are you okay, Daddy? Were you dreaming?"

"No, sweetie. I was meditating. I guess it is sort of like dreaming."

"You were smiling a lot," she informs me.

"Oh really? I suppose I probably was. I was thinking about good things," I explain.

She smiles. "Oh good."

I return her smile.

"Daddy, are you going to read me a story and tuck me in?"

"Absolutely, my dear. What story would you like?"

She stops to think for a moment then her face lights up. "How about One Fish. Two Fish?"

"Dr. Seuss?" I confirm.

She nods enthusiastically.

"You got it, Kiddo. Let's go!" I love all the Dr. Seuss books, but especially that one. I keep it to myself that whenever she says "One Fish. Two Fish," the voice in my head always completes it with ,"Three fish, four fish, five fish. Now let's head to weigh-in!"

Ch 17
Looking Up

My boss Greg follows me into my office and closes the door behind us. "That was excellent work in there, William," he tells me in reference to the boardroom we just left. "I think the big guys were pretty impressed."

"Oh, thanks. The answer just seemed logical to me," I respond humbly.

"Well, they've been struggling with that for six months. I'm not sure why they've always gone to Cutler for their big projects. You're twice the programmer he is. Maybe now they'll see that," he tells me sincerely.

"Wow. Thanks, Greg. That's really nice of you to say."

"I speak the truth," he says, holding his arms outstretched to his sides as if to prove that he has nothing to hide. Then it looks as if something just occurred to him. He squints his eyes and focuses all his attention on me, like he's looking for a clue. "It really seems like you've been extra sharp lately."

"I feel great," I confirm.

I can see that he's trying to think of the right way to phrase what he wants to say. "Don't get your hopes up, like I'm coming on to you or something," he kids, "but you've lost some weight, haven't you?"

I laugh and shake my head. "I guess. Maybe 15 or 20 pounds," I tell him, trying to sound like it's no big deal.

"New diet? Did the wife sign you up?" he asks playfully.

"Really, I've just been exercising and generally taking better care of myself."

He hesitates for a second and decides to accept this as a reasonable answer. "Well, whatever it is, keep it up." He ends his sentence with a cheesy thumbs up.

I smile and return the thumb.

"Alright," he confirms as our conversation winds down. He turns, opens the door and heads out to the hall. "Again, excellent job, William." He pauses to be sure we make eye contact.

"Thanks, Greg."

Then he remembers one more thing. "Oh, I got an email from the International Programming Language Conference coming up in a couple weeks. Are you familiar with it?"

I nod. "I've heard of it. That's a pretty big conference."

"Well, I guess it's in Chicago this year. If you think it would be worthwhile, I'd like to send you," he offers.

"Hmm. That might be something."

"I'll forward that email. You check it out and let me know if you're interested." I smile. "I'll do that. Thanks."

"Thank you, William. Nice job." With that, he closes the door.

I really have noticed that work seems easier for me lately. I think the job is the same as it has always been, I just find it easier to stay on course with my projects and not let the little things derail me anymore. Plus, my confidence has never been higher.

My home life seems to be better than it's been in years. I mean, it has always been pretty good, but I have fewer unpleasant moments. I feel reconnected with Trixie, and I get the impression that she feels closer to me too. We haven't talked about it specifically, but I can feel it. Obviously, she knows that I've been studying and working out, but we've really only talked about how it all relates to my fishing.

Actually, I guess I've done most of the fishing talk, she just listens kindly. I think the most likely contributor to my improved relationship with my wife is my conscious and consistent focus on the things for which I am grateful. I start each day by listing five things I am grateful for. I picture each thing on my list and really focus my feelings of gratitude toward that thing. Trixie and Dacey always account for two of the five things. Come to think of it, my job, which allows me to provide for my family, usually ends up on the list too. Maybe that's part of the reason for my increased performance here. Ooh, and speaking of that, I'd better get back to work.

Ch 18
The Ex

The big glass automatic door slides open and I spot Cam just beyond a menacing, nine-foot-tall, grizzly bear.

"Hey, Buck! Glad you could make it," he calls to me.

"Hey, Cam! Thanks for the invite," I respond and shake the hand he offers. "I'm always up for wandering around the aisles of a Gander Mountain store on a Sunday afternoon."

"I figured," he smiles.

"Oh, and before I forget, here's the money for those reels." I hand him a stack of 20s folded in half.

He gives me an awkward look and quickly tucks the cash into his coat pocket. "Is there anything specific you're looking for?" he inquires, trying to put the last 10 seconds way behind us.

"I thought I'd check out some new line. I've got a list of what I need," I tell him and pat the folded note paper in my front shirt pocket.

"Cool. I thought I'd stock up on jigs, if they have what I want."

I nod my approval.

"Well let's head that way," he instructs, and turns away from the big grizzly.

Together, we head toward the fishing equipment. I decide to make some small talk. "So, any word on your boat?"

He breathes an audible sigh and says, "Nope."

Seems like a touchy subject. I know how frustrating boats can be. "Well, if it comes down to it, we can definitely use my boat for the team tourneys, and if you needed to borrow it for yourself, I would..."

"Thanks," he replies sharply, cutting me off in mid-generosity. "I'm sure I'll get my boat problem figured out soon."

I can't tell if he's upset that I brought it up. I guess I really don't know him well enough to get a read on him. I'm going to assume that he thought my offer was honest and well-intentioned. He's a bit tough to figure out. No wonder it's taken me all these years to get on his good side. Maybe I should change the subject.

"So what jigs do you use?" I ask casually, as if the boat talk had never happened.

"Well, it depends. I really like All-terrain for a good general pitching and flipping jig. Seems to work pretty well in just about any cover. But for serious wood cover I stick with the old classic Strike King Denny Brauer model."

"Mmm hmm," I nod. "I've used them both quite a bit." Pretty standard answers, I think to myself. I guess that's good. He's approaching it logically. He knows what works, but he's not getting too fancy.

"You got any favorite colors?" he asks.

Hmm, kind of an elementary question. Maybe he's testing me. "Well, it's funny you should ask." Here's a chance for me to impress him with my advanced understanding of fishing. I know he already said we're partners, but now I can reassure him that he's made a good choice. Yes, I realize this line of thinking is silly, but here goes. "I've been reading a book by the head scientist at Pure Fishing. It's called *Knowing Bass*. Have you read it?"

116

He shakes his head no.

"Well, it's been a real eye-opener. This guy's been studying bass in a controlled, accurate, scientific setting so he's presenting real facts instead of wive's tales and assumptions."

Cam looks interested, but I think I detect a bit of defensiveness.

I continue. "For example, a bass' eye is physically different than our eye. They can't see nearly as wide of a color spectrum as we can. Their ability to recognize colors from red to green is good, but falls off quickly outside of that range. All the shades of purple and blue are most likely perceived as just dark, rather than specific colors."

I pause to take a breath. Cam has one eyebrow raised. "So what's the best color?" he demands.

"It's tough to say for sure, because in a test where fish were presented the same lure painted different colors, red and orange–the colors they should see best– were the least frequently bit."

"So, what color was most frequently bit?" he asks a bit impatiently.

"In that test, purple was the best solid color," I tell him.

"So, purple?"

"Kind of," I respond with a bit less confidence. It is becoming obvious to me that he's not finding this as fascinating as I did. "You see, they also threw a silver with black back lure into the mix, and the fish showed a huge preference to that over the other colors."

He doesn't respond this time, making sure I'm completely done.

I'm already in this deep, so I may as well finish the lesson. "Then mix in the

117

properties of light and color as they pass through water and it really messes things up. In stained water, red, orange and yellow are about the only colors that can even exist. And after so many feet, they disappear too."

Still no response.

"So the scientist concluded that color is probably much less important than a lot of other factors in triggering a strike. He recommends focusing on contrast and how well your lure will show up against its background." I smile sheepishly. "Interesting stuff, though. You should read that book. Really made me think."

"Yea, that sounds interesting," he agrees. "So, pumpkin and green melon should be good choices?"

"Oh, um, well sure. They're in that part of the spectrum bass can see, so sure. Good as any," I smile again. I breathe a little sigh of relief. Once I got rolling, I realized that I may be coming across as a "know it all". I guess I did want to "razzle dazzle" him a bit, but mostly I was just sharing something I found interesting and beneficial.

"As long as I can still use pumpkin," he chuckles as he pulls several 1/2 once pumpkin colored jigs from the display and tosses them into his basket.

"Let me know if you want to borrow that book," I offer.

"Yeah, sounds good. I think I would check that out, Buck."

"Done," I respond with a smile.

"Okay. Let's go see what you can teach me about fishing line," he kids.

I round the corner of the fishing reel counter and BOOM–I find myself face to face with Doug. Oh crap.

"Doug! What are you doing here?" I manage awkwardly.

"I come here for the fresh-baked scones and live jazz music," he answers cooly. "What are you doing here?"

"Jazz music," I chuckle uncomfortably. "Always the comedian. Oh, I'm just here to pick up some line."

I see his eyes spot Cam behind me. "With Cam," I declare as if Doug will be excited to see him. I step to the side, revealing my new buddy to my betrayed old buddy.

"Hey, Doug," Cam says friendly enough.

"Cam," he nods.

Cam looks at the reel Doug has been holding since we found him. "I've never had much luck with Daiwa, myself."

We all look at the reel in Doug's hands. Obviously there's nothing wrong with Daiwa reels but he sets it back on the counter as if it's on fire.

"Yeah, me too," he tells Cam. "I'm just checking things out–not really ready to buy."

"I've been a Shimano guy for a long time," Cam offers.

"Hard to go wrong with Shimano," Doug agrees, then he looks at me. "Didn't you say you were thinking about switching away from Shimano this year, William?" It was true. We had discussed it towards the end of last season. *Thanks, Doug,* I think to myself.

"Um, I'm gonna stick with Shimano," I try to sound confident.

"Oh?" he asks.

"Yeah, I picked up a couple new Chronarchs already, so I'm pretty set for this season," I inform Doug.

"Wow. Two new Chronarchs?" He does that whistle that guys do to show they're impressed. "Trixie must have increased your fishing budget this year," he elbows me to punctuate his ribbing.

"Yeah, Cam found a pretty great deal on them," I tell him with a forced obligatory laugh.

"Well, hey. It was great to see you, Doug. Good luck this season," Cam brings our meeting to an abrupt end. He steps around us both and continues our trek to the fishing line aisle.

Cam's actions stun us both for a second.

"Um, yeah. We're gonna go check out lines," I reach out to shake Doug's hand. He accepts cordially but a bit hesitantly. "We'll talk soon," I tell him insincerely over my shoulder as I hustle to catch up with Cam.

Sheesh, that was awkward–like running into an ex-girlfriend while I'm out with my wife. Actually, Doug was well-behaved. I don't know. I guess any feelings of guilt are my own creation. I still like Doug. Hell, I love Doug. He's my brother, and he's always been a very close friend. I mean, he has been kind of jerky about my new direction, but I guess I'm the one who's changed. He really hasn't done anything wrong. I need to fish a tournament with Cam...soon.

Ch 19
Clearing The Air

"No, I'm not accusing you of anything," Trixie says firmly. "I'm just wondering if you and Doug had some kind of falling out."

"Why? What did he tell you?" I try to turn it away from me.

"He hasn't said a word," she insists as she pulls a stool back from the counter and has a seat. "In fact, he seems fine. I just know that in years past, you've spent a lot of time in his garage working on fishing stuff. Now, unless you're sneaking over there behind my back, which doesn't make any sense, I don't think you've been to his house in months. That's all."

"Oh, I don't think it's been months," I counter weakly. She makes a face that lets me know she believes otherwise.

"Look, it's fine with me. I was just curious," she says defensively, then explains, "If there was a problem, I just didn't want to say something to him that might make things worse."

"Nope. No problem," I declare innocently. "Doug and I are still friends, as far as I know."

Trixie relaxes her guard a bit. "Well good. I know you guys always have so much fun fishing together. It would be a shame if that had to stop."

"Yeah," I mumble, "a shame." I break eye contact with her and look at the floor.

"Seems like there's more you'd like to say," she insists.

I hate not being open and honest with her.

"It's just...well, he...Doug doesn't believe that the mental aspects of...well, Cam has a long history of tournament success and he..."

Trixie waits patiently for me to finish my thought.

"I really do miss hanging around with Doug." I'm pleased with myself for forming a complete sentence. "Doug is my friend. He's my brother. We always have fun together." She nods in agreement. "It's just with all the effort I've been putting into my new approach, I really want it to pay off next year. I've got an opportunity to fish tournaments with a guy who's way more accomplished than Doug or myself. If I fish with Cam as my partner, I'm really going to have a shot at winning several tournaments."

When I hear myself say it out loud, it really sounds bad. Not only does it sound bad, it feels bad. I've betrayed my closest friend to win a couple small-time tournaments with a guy who I really don't know. It occurs to me that Cam really doesn't answer many personal questions. *Why does he go through so many partners?* Then the sweet, but highly suspicious Chronarch reels come to mind. I know that I shouldn't jump to any conclusions, so I push the thought out of my mind. Maybe I should be saying some of these thoughts out loud so I can get some feedback from my beautiful, understanding wife. She's staring at me. But I know her well enough to understand that her look is not judgmental. It is a look that says she's there for me. She supports me and she knows I will come to the right conclusion if she just gives me time and encouragement.

I clear my throat. "It really does bother me that I haven't been honest with Doug."

"Have you been dishonest with him?" Trixie asks with concern.

"No, not really. Maybe. I don't know. I mean, I've been more evasive than dishonest."

"Hmm," she responds. She wants me to keep talking.

"I really did decide on this plan at the end of last season, but since then I've done a lot of studying–a lot of growing. I really think it's changed more than just my fishing." Trixie nods her agreement. "But it seems so obvious to me now that I've been focused on the wrong prize," I continue. "Although, Cam seems like a good guy, doesn't he?" I look to her for approval.

"I really don't know him, William. I can't remember him ever saying anything more than hello and goodbye to me. I guess he wasn't rude, I just don't know much about him. I don't think I even know where he lives."

"He's just over in Cadott, right off the highway," I explain.

"Oh, Cadott? Does he know my cousin Amy, or maybe Connor? I was just talking with her today."

"I'm not sure," I confess. I'm a bit embarrassed that I hadn't really thought about the fact that her cousin lived in the same town as Cam. "He's never mentioned them."

"She said there was a fire right up the street from her today."

"A fire? Yikes! Everyone okay?"

"Amy didn't know. I think she said it was a garage, not a house. Did Cam say anything about it?" she asks.

"No. Actually, I haven't talked to him in a couple days. Maybe I should give him a call just to make sure everything is okay."

"Probably not a bad idea," she agrees.

I reach into my pocket and grab my phone. Then I realize Trixie is watching me.

"So, have you decided what you're going to do? Did this help?" she asks sincerely.

I step forward and wrap my arms around her. "Thank you," I whisper in her ear. "Everything is going to be just fine."

Ch 20
Repairing The Bridge

Rather than head upstairs to my office, I head out to the garage–to my other office. There's nothing better than standing on the front deck of my trusty Ranger, floating around on a warm, summer morning, but there is something very cool about hanging out in the boat while it's parked in the garage. I find privacy here. I find it easier to focus on fishing-related topics here. I've even taken to meditating out here on occasion. The sweet smell of PowerBait mixed with two-stroke oil really helps my visualization exercises.

Once comfy in the passenger seat, I take my iPhone out of my pocket. I'm about to dial Cam's number when I notice a voice message from Doug.

"How did I miss that?" I mumble to myself as I press play to hear the message.

"Um, hey. It's Doug, your brother-in-law. Um...give me a call, you know, when you get a chance. Um, okay. Thanks. Bye," said the recording.

Well, that wasn't a typical Doug message, I think to myself. *You know what, William? It's time to set things right. Cam can wait. Call Doug back right now.*

I highlight his voicemail and press the call back button. It rings once and I sit up straight and clear my throat. I'm suddenly excited about the possibility of taking care of this right now. This whole situation has been haunting me for the past couple months.

"Hey, William," Doug greets me with a chipper voice.

"Hey, Doug," I respond. "How's it going?"

"Not too bad. How about you?" he replies cordially.

"Okay, thanks."

"Good! Hey, I wanted to ask you about..."

"Doug! Hold on a second. I don't mean to cut you off, but I've got something I really need to talk about first."

"Oh...okay," he responds a bit surprised. "Sure. What have you got, William?"

I clear my throat again. "Doug..." I hesitate briefly, but quickly decide to follow through. Here goes. "Doug, I've been an ass. I have not been treating you like a best friend. I was pissed that you weren't open to my new ideas about fishing, but that's no excuse for my behavior," I pause but Doug does not respond. I continue, "I made some bad decisions for the wrong reasons. I've just been fishing these tournaments for so long without reaching the level I know I'm capable of, but I shouldn't have blamed you for my lack of success. I thought I had an opportunity to get what I wanted, but I can see now that I was after the wrong thing." I pause again. *I think that was what I wanted to say. Alright, let's see how Doug takes all that.*

After a second of silence, he chuckles and simply says, "Wow."

"Wow?" I wonder aloud.

"I mean," he clarifies, "I get the part where you're an ass, but as for the rest I have no idea what you're talking about." He chuckles again. "Seriously, William, I don't mean to make light of it because you seem pretty worked up, but I really don't understand."

My knee-jerk reaction would be to snap at him. *I'm pouring my heart out and he's laughing. But that's the old William. New William remains calm and stays focused. Of course he doesn't understand,* I remind myself. *I've been doing all this planning behind his back.*

"The thing is, Doug, I've made plans to fish the team tournaments with Cam this summer."

"Oh...yeah, I guessed that might be happening," he responds calmly.

"Well, in any case, I should have just told you the truth."

He laughs, "I probably wouldn't have taken that news very well."

I laugh with him. "Look, I just want to tell you I'm sorry. I've been an idiot and I hope we can put this behind us."

"Idiot? I thought you were an ass?" Doug teases.

"Fair enough," I concede.

"So, are you still planning to do the tournaments with Cam?" he asks.

"I told him I would, but I'm torn. If you're still available, I'd like to find a way to fish with you," I answer sincerely.

"Well, two things, brother," Doug says with some hesitation, "I've made plans to partner up with my cousin Amy's husband, Connor."

"Oh, I see," I try to sound calm, but that really catches me off guard.

"And second, I think Cam may need you for your boat," he says matter-of-factly.

"Need me for my boat?" I demand.

"Oh, you haven't talked to him?" Doug asks sheepishly.

"No. What have you heard?"

"Um, well...I was over at Connor's earlier, and when I went by Cam's place I couldn't help but notice there had been a fire."

"Seriously!? That was at Cam's house? Trixie just told me there was a fire in Cadott, but she didn't know whose house it was. I was just about to call him."

"Yep. I saw him out front with a couple guys from the fire station. He looked like he was alright, but the garage was completely gone. It was weird to see the charred, melted blob of a boat on the trailer with all four tires burned off just sitting there where the garage used to be."

"Holy crap," I respond. "Did you talk to him?"

"No, he looked pretty distracted. Once I saw that he was okay, I thought I should let him focus on the problem at hand."

"Sure. I suppose," I agree. "Wow! This is all so weird."

"Yeah, it's pretty weird when you see something like that. I know I double-checked my battery charger when I got home. I actually felt it to make sure it wasn't warm."

"Yeah. Can't be too safe," I add.

"Well, hey, you should probably give him a call and make sure everything's okay," Doug suggests with genuine concern in his voice. "Tell him I'm sorry to hear what happened but I'm glad he's all right."

"Of course. Will do." I pause, trying to decide if I need to say anything more about my apology to Doug.

He doesn't give me the chance. "Cool! I'll talk to you soon, William."

"I'm looking forward to it, Doug. Bye."

I press the big red button to end the call, smile, and lean back into the comfortable, familiar boat seat. I'm so glad I finally manned up and faced that. I think he made it pretty easy on me. I guess I'm not surprised. That's the calm, non-confrontational way he handles most things. That's exactly what I've missed about our friendship. I've had some decent times with Cam, but he's...well...wound a little tighter. He's more intense. He's pretty much the opposite of Doug. *Cam! I need to call Cam,* I remember. A few quick taps and the call is on its way.

"Yello?" a surprisingly upbeat voice answers.

"Cam? Hey, it's William."

"Hey, what's up, Buck?" he asks like it's just a normal day.

"Oh, not much here, but I heard you had a pretty...um, exciting day at your house."

"What? Oh, the fire? Yeah, that was crazy," he said as if that was all that needed to be said.

I was a bit stunned at his casual demeanor. "Well, are you okay? I mean, what happened?"

"Yep. Fine. They're not sure what happened. Maybe an electrical fire? Maybe some punk kids did it? The fire department is trying to figure it out, but I have a feeling they may never know for sure."

"Really? Maybe arson? Is there anybody who would do that to you? Have you had any other problems with the kids in your neighborhood?" I ask with concern. That's the same neighborhood where Trixie's cousin lives.

"You know, there are punk-ass kids everywhere these days. No respect for anybody's property," he says, finally with a bit of emotion in his voice. "But, what are ya gonna do?" he asks rhetorically.

"I guess...sad, though. Glad you're okay. Sorry to hear about your boat."

I wait, assuming he'll offer the obligatory "thank you", but he says nothing.

"Alright then," I say to fill the void, "I guess I'll let you go. I imagine you've got plenty to work on. Um, let me know if there's anything I can do to help," I offer.

He finally responds, but his voice is ice cold. "Will do, Buck, but like I told you, I was sure I'd get it taken care of one way or another."

I'm not sure how to respond, but I don't really need to.

"Talk to you soon," he says, and hangs up.

I sit alone in my boat in my garage. I hold my iPhone out in front of me and watch a photo of Cam holding a big crappie as it's replaced by the words "call ended" and then fades back to my home screen. "What did he mean by that?" Like a lot of things Cam has said, I remind myself not to jump to conclusions. *I wonder why I have to keep reminding myself of that with him. One way or another? I ask myself. That seems pretty thinly veiled. Alright, William. That next thought you're about to have is pretty serious. Slow down. Try focusing on your breath for a minute. Close your eyes, clear your thoughts and reset.*

Breathe in. One. Two. Three. Four.

Breathe out. One. Two. Three. Four. Five. Six.

I open my eyes, and the first thing I see is my two new Chronarch reels mounted on my favorite St. Croix rods lying on the front deck.

Half price? I ask myself with disgust. *One way or another?* I rub my forehead with my hand. *He has a feeling they may never know for sure what happened?* I pick up a scrap PitBoss Craw from the bottom of my boat and throw it toward the garbage can. *Am I naive? Am I blind?* I can't seem to get my brain to say the words insurance fraud or arson or thief, but my heart can feel it. I swallow hard and finally accept what I've known for quite a while. *Cam and I are not going to be partners. I'm pretty sure we're not even going to be friends.*

Ch 21
My Subconscious Knows

It's warm, calm and still dark, but I can see surprisingly well. Water laps gently against the hull of my fiberglass boat as I use my electric trolling motor to move into position.

I scan the rods laid out on the deck and select a topwater bait I don't think I've ever seen before. It's got to be twice as big as any popper I've ever thrown before–a good eight to ten inches long, and as big around as a banana. How am I going to be able to cast this beast with my bass rod, I wonder. I unhook it from the reel and let it swing from the tip of the rod back to my free hand. It's surprisingly light. It appears to be made of some sort of tough, soft foam. Cool!

As the water moves slowly around a bend in this slough, it doubles back on itself, forming a huge eddy. I pull the boat into a slack-water area just down-stream from the vortex. Suddenly, a huge school of fleeing baitfish erupts on the surface just ahead, startling me and causing me to jump back. "Oh, they're here," I laugh nervously.

I stand motionless, like a hunting tiger waiting to spring on its prey. "Show yourself," I hiss tauntingly. Night is all around me. Without warning, there's a huge splash–I even think I hear a gulping noise–there at 11 o' clock in the giant whirlpool in front of me.

I load the rod over my shoulder and sling my giant lure into the darkness toward the commotion. For such a large presentation, it touches down with barely a splash. I jerk the rod tip down and the big plug slashes and gurgles violently.

"Wow, that looks awesome!" my partner reassures me from the back of the boat.

I twitch it again and the banana jumps and pops to life. The current is washing it around the edge of the eddy. I reel the slack from my line and give it another snap, but there is no sound this time. Then I realize my line is cutting off in the opposite direction of the current.

"He's got it!" my partner shouts. "Set the hook!"

I rear back and feel the distinct head shake of a powerful fish. "Got him!" I exclaim. "Got him!" Line peels off in the opposite direction as I strain to tighten the reel's drag system. Ahead of me in the darkness, the fish surfaces with the giant yellow plug in its mouth. Actually, I can't really see the fish, but I can't miss that lure.

Fairly quickly, I manage to guide the fish out of the current and into the slack water near my boat. "Get ready with that net!" I call.

My partner bumps into me as we stand shoulder to shoulder on the front deck. "I'll get him," he assures me. "Just play him easy. Don't horse him," he coaches.

I can see the yellow lure just at the side of the boat. "Get him, Johnny! Get him!"

I can hear his bracelets and jewelry rattling and clanging as his puffy white sleeve extends fully with the net.

"Got him!" he cries as he lifts the net into the boat.

"Thanks, Johnny Depp," I tell him sincerely. "Nice net."

"No problem, but call me Captain Jack if you please," he requests.

"Of course," I readily agree. He winks at me and I smile excitedly.

"Let's see what ye got," he reminds me and motions to the net.

"Of course. My fish," I say somewhat embarrassed. I reach into the net and grab a nice, although fairly unimpressive, three-pound largemouth bass by its bottom lip.

"Tis a beauty, Buck!" he shouts.

I don't want to upset him, but I don't think this fish is even big enough to bother with a photo. I hold it up, doubting my own assessment. Maybe it's bigger than I thought.

"I hate to be the bearer of bad tidings," Captain Jack tells me seriously, "but I really think we should head for the nearest port."

"What? Why?" I demand, "We're just getting started."

"I'm afraid this vessel isn't seaworthy," he says and motions with his hands to see for myself.

Thick, dark smoke is all around us. I choke on the harsh, toxic, burning-plastic vapor. Beneath my feet is a black, bubbling, charcoal version of my former Ranger.

"Oh my God, Johnny," I shout. "How did this happen?"

Johnny Depp looks me right in the eye. His frilly clothes and long, scraggly hair are blowing in the hot air. Without a hint of panic, he tells me, "I have a feeling we may never know for sure."

"William, are you all right?" Trixie asks.

Wait, Trixie is at home. How did she...

135

"William! Are you all right?" she tries again.

I sit up in bed abruptly. Trixie narrowly escapes a serious head butt.

"You were dreaming, dear," she tries to calm me. "Are you okay? You look a bit rattled."

As my brain begins to grasp reality, I take a deep breath and try to relax. "Yeah, I'm fine." I smile sheepishly. "Just a weird dream."

"Do you want to talk about it?" she offers.

I pause for a second to collect my thoughts. "I think I was fishing with Johnny Depp," I tell her.

"Well that doesn't sound so bad to me," she giggles.

I chuckle with her. "Well, it was weird," I promise.

"Hmm. I think I might try to have that dream," she teases, then kisses me on the forehead.

I sigh and give her a playful, mock-disgusted look.

She smiles and lays back down on her pillow. "Try to have sweet dreams, dear. Love you."

"Love you too. I'll try," I respond. "Sorry I woke you."

I recline and stare at the ceiling. I need to let Cam know we're done...soon.

Ch 22
Make The Call

My phone buzzes with the third text message from Cam in as many minutes. I try to focus on work, but it's going to be challenging today. There's just too much on my mind. I really think I need to cut ties with Cam before I find some undeniable proof of his wrongdoing. So far, I just have my own suspicion. I think I'd rather hope that I'm all wrong and get out now before I'm obligated to go to the police.

The phone buzzes again. Reluctantly, I hold it up in front of myself like it's an angry snake ready to bite or an M-80 ready to explode. With my head turned to the side and my eyes squinted nearly shut, I allow the message to come into my peripheral vision. *Please don't be evidence,* I beg.

"Getting new boat on Saturday. Picking up in La Crosse," reads the text.

"Wow, that didn't take long," I think to myself. With a sigh, I picture my 10-year-old boat at home.

I drag my finger across the screen to reveal the other messages.

"Got a minute to talk?"

"Hello? Big news!"

"Problem solved."

I'm not sure what the appropriate response is. I stare at the text screen. I guess these comments aren't incriminating. If it were anyone else, I would say it seems perfectly normal. For a moment, I wonder if I am all wrong, then I find my resolve. It doesn't matter. This just isn't going to work. Is there an easy way to get out? Obviously, I would prefer to avoid a big blowout. How can I tell him I've decided to change the plans we'd made because I think he is a lying crook?

I type the words, "We need to talk," and just stare at them. Delete, delete, delete. I type "Congrats" and hit send. That doesn't feel right I admit to myself, but I haven't figured out how I want to handle this yet.

Bzzz. Bzzz. "Wanna come with on Saturday?"

I let my head flop back, eyes closed but pointed straight up at the ceiling and let out a low, slow groan.

"You okay, Buckner?" I hear Ian's obnoxious voice ask.

I pretend to turn my misery into a stretch. My groan morphs to a growly sort of yawn. "Rrrrr. Wooooo. Oh, hey Ian. What's up?" I ask innocently.

"Just passing by and thought you may be dying," he smiles then laughs.

"No such luck," I counter and he laughs even harder.

The laughter fades quickly and we're left face to face with an awkward silence.

"I sure am ready for spring," he offers.

"Yep. It's been a long winter," I reply politely.

"You gonna be fishing over on the river this summer?"

"I've got my first tournament of the year over in Wabasha in mid-May," I inform him. I thought about just saying "yes" but I was afraid then he'd just come up with some new topic. At least this way we're talking about fishing.

"Wabasha? Boy, I used to spend a lot of time there as a kid," he says as if he's ramping up to his famous story about white bass.

"Yeah, you've mentioned that. You used to catch a lot of white bass." I let him know I've heard this one before.

"Oh, white bass you wouldn't believe," he continues anyway.

I nod.

"We really should get out there together this year," he suggests with a big smile. His eyebrows are raised high waiting for my answer.

"Sounds like a plan," I tell him.

"Boy, I'll show you a thing or two about catching white bass," he brags.

"Promise?" I ask with fake enthusiasm that he must believe to be genuine.

"Deal," he says. Then he laughs at apparently nothing, knocks twice on the front corner of my desk, and marches directly out of my office.

While that conversation did allow me to put off thinking about the Cam situation for a couple minutes, I don't feel any better.

Bzzz. Bzzz. "Well?"

I stare at the screen. *Maybe I'll go with him on Saturday. We'd have plenty of time in the truck for me to figure out a graceful exit strategy. Unfortunately, then I'm also in the moving vehicle of a guy who I don't trust so he can stab me and dump me in the river.* I laugh at myself for jumping to murderer so quickly. *Alright, he probably wouldn't stab me, but those would sure be some uncomfortable miles.*

I type, "Sorry. Can't do this weekend."

I wait for a response but my phone isn't buzzing. The break gives me time to think about this rationally. So far, my reactions to Cam have been very knee-jerk. I sit up straight in my desk chair and focus on my breath. I feel a calmness begin to wash over me. Much better. Now, I begin to review what I know about Cam. *Wait a second,* I tell myself. *You're not married to him, William. We're dudes. Just gradually put some distance between us and the problem will disappear.* For some reason I've been picturing some big, painful, potentially deadly, breakup. The fact is, the only commitment I've made to him is for the team tournament. If I back out now he'll have nearly two months to find someone else. Maybe he'll prefer to fish with someone else. I don't love the idea of going back on my word, but I think it will be best to make this exception.

There. That wasn't so hard. I shift in my chair and try to get a read on how I feel. *Better, but still not great. Of course not,* I realize. *It's still hanging over my head. I need to take action and take care of this–the sooner, the better.*

I clear my throat, pull my shoulders back, and dial Cam's number.

"Hey, Buck," he answers almost immediately.

"Hey, Cam," I reply calmly. "So new boat already, huh?"

"Yeah, I was gonna order direct from the factory, but I found a pretty sweet boat on the showroom floor in La Crosse. I'm having the marina make a few changes, adding a few goodies before I pick it up this weekend," he informs me.

"Nice," I respond. I think that sounded sincere.

"So, I saw you're not going to be able to ride down with me?"

"Yeah, I'm going to spend the weekend with the girls. You know, I like to get my family time in before open water." Not untrue, I tell myself.

"Sure. To each his own," he says in a kidding tone of voice, but I can't tell if he's kidding. "You'll have to sneak over one evening next week and check it out. You'll want to see how big the back deck is on this thing. It's like a dance floor!"

Here we go, I think to myself. "Hey, Cam. That reminds me, I've been meaning to talk to you about those team tournaments."

I feel his playful enthusiasm disappear. "What about them, William?" he asks in that super-calm, steady voice that evil, crazy, bad guys use in Bond movies.

"Well...I'm afraid I'm not going to be able to fish them with you this year." *There. I said it. Not so bad.* Then I realize he hasn't responded. I'm not sure if it's nerves or just a need to fill the uncomfortable silence, but I continue. "I hope that doesn't put you in a bad spot. I would guess with two months notice you should be able..."

"Unbelievable," he cuts me off in a slightly raised voice.

I try again. "Maybe I could help you find someone who..."

"Are you serious?" he demands. Then slightly louder, "Are you serious?"

"Well, I just..."

"You think I just randomly pick someone to gamble my entry money on? Finding the right partner for these events takes time!" he shouts.

"But there's still two..."

"C'mon, Bill! It takes more than two months! This is unbelievable!"

I gladly let the whole Bill-William thing slide. I can hear his breathing becoming beast-like between rants. *Yikes! I knew this guy was unstable. I can't wait for this to be over.*

"Do you have any idea what I've gone through to make sure we have a good boat to fish from?"

I decide not to answer that question.

"What, are you going back to Doug? Well good luck with that! How's that teammate worked out for you so far?"

"What? No. Look, Doug has nothing to do with this," I finally counter a bit. "Unbelievable. Just unbelievable!" he shouts.

"Cam, I certainly didn't want to put you in a bad spot with these tournaments, but the thing is..." I swallow hard and find my courage. "I just don't think you and I make a good team. I'm sure you're a good fisherman, but I don't feel like I know if you're a good man." *Wow, that did sound quite a bit like a breakup speech,* I think to myself.

Then it dawns on me that he hasn't responded and I don't hear his insane breathing. *That's odd.* I hold the phone out in front of me. The display reads, "Call ended."

Ch 23
Karma's Scorecard

"There's no need to complicate, our time is short. This is our fate,
I'm your-or-or-o-o-orsss."

I catch Dacey's eye reflected in my rearview mirror. She smiles sweetly from
her booster seat and pretends like she wasn't just singing along with the radio.

"How do you know this song?" I inquire.

She pauses trying to decide if she's going to deny singing along. I suppose,
based on my playful, non-accusatory tone it's obviously okay to own up to it.

"Mommy listens to Jason The Raz all the time," she tells me as confidently as
she can muster.

The Raz? I struggle to not laugh. "Oh, that's right," I smile, "she does like him."
She looks out the window and continues singing. The words she's unsure of
are soft, almost mumbled, but the words she knows well are quite a bit louder.

"Thanks for coming with on my errands, Kiddo. You're good company."
She smiles her acknowledgement. "And a good singer," I add. She smiles
even brighter.

I pull into a parking space and put the truck in park. Then I wait until the
song ends before removing the key.

Together Dacey and I walk hand-in-hand across the parking lot, past the
giant grizzly bear, and straight to the reel counter. Almost immediately we're
greeted by a pleasant, eager young man.

"Is there something I can help you find today?" he asks.

"No, actually I have kind of a...strange situation, I'm hoping you can help me with," I begin.

"I'll sure try," he promises. "What have you got?"

"Well, about a month or so ago, a friend of mine picked up a couple fishing reels for me." I reach into a plastic shopping bag and set the pair of Chronarch/Citica on the glass display case between us.

"Uh, huh," he lets me know he's staying with me.

"Well, I think he may have been...um, undercharged and I'd like to make sure that the store received fair compensation."

His nose crinkles up a bit. I'm sure this is a new one for him. "Do you have your receipt?" he asks politely.

"No, I'm afraid I don't have a receipt."

He looks like he might already be out of ideas.

"Were they on sale recently?" I ask. I know it's a long shot, but maybe Cam was telling the truth.

"Hmmm. Maybe," he responds, then starts typing on his computer. "Well here are this week's sale items...hmm. No...Well, maybe if we check..." His face looks strained and puzzled, and he begins typing again.

Dacey is happily spinning the handles on all of the display model reels.

"Is there any way to look up purchases by name?" I ask even though I realize there probably isn't.

"Not really without that receipt," he explains.

"Well, how much do Chronarchs cost, because maybe I can just pay the difference."

Now he looks like he doesn't know how to help me and he suspects that I may be crazy. "Sir, I'm not sure where I would even enter a transaction like that."

"No, I guess not," I admit.

"Are you dissatisfied with the reels?" he wonders.

"Well, no, not at all."

He offers me a reassuring smile. "Well then I would suggest that you enjoy them. I haven't been informed of any problems with reel sales. I think everything is fine."

I don't think I've accomplished anything, but I understand that there may not be any way to make things right here. I think about it for a couple seconds then I nod. "Yes. Okay. Well, thank you for trying," I reassure him.

"Sorry I couldn't be more helpful with that," he says sincerely. "Is there anything else I can help you find, today?"

"Um, no. I think that will do it. Thanks." I turn from the counter. "Okay, Dace. Time to go."

Okay, Daddy. Is everything alright?" she asks, reading my face.

I remember to smile. "Absolutely, dear. We just need to make one more stop.

* * *

The time printed on the door says they should be open, but the door is locked.

145

"I don't think anyone is here," Dacey informs me.

"The lights are on in that office down the hall," I point through the locked glass double door keeping us out. "And the sign says they should be open."

"Yeah, but still," she says, and pulls on the door handle.

"Maybe I should knock," I suggest, not really looking for her approval. I give the glass three solid raps with my knuckles. A few seconds later, a woman's head peeks out of the office. When she sees us waiting there, her face lights up like we were old friends she hadn't seen in years.

"Oh, just a minute," she calls in a sing-songy voice as she heads down the hall. She's very sweet looking–mid-60s, a little overweight, casually dressed but well put together–very grandmotherly. "I'm sorry. I didn't know it was locked." She smiles warmly as she turns the deadbolt with a solid, metallic, industrial click.

"Good morning," she greets us. "How may I help you?"

"Good morning," we both respond. Then I ask, "I'm wondering if this would be the right place to make a donation of sporting equipment for the children?"

"Perhaps, dear. What exactly do you want to donate?"

"Well, I believe the park district organizes programs teaching fishing to underprivileged kids. Is that still true?"

"Oh, absolutely," she assures me. "Last year was our best turnout ever. There were nearly twenty children enrolled. It's becoming very popular."

"Great. Well, I would like to donate these fishing reels to the program," I smile and hold the bag out to her.

"Oh, how wonderful!" she exclaims. "That's very generous of you." Then her smile fades. "Have you given up fishing?" she asks with a great deal of concern.

"What? Oh, no. I still do a lot of fishing–tournament fishing. In fact, my first bass tournament of the season is in May. I just thought the children might need these more than I do."

Her smile returns. "Very generous, indeed. I don't suppose you would..." She lets her thought trail off.

"I would what?"

She hesitates for a second, then continues. "I don't want to seem like I'm taking advantage of your generosity, but I wonder if you, as such an accomplished fisherman, might be interested in donating your skills to teaching some of our classes?"

"Oh, I don't know about accomplished," I blush.

"You're going to teach other kids how to fish?" Dacey asks enthusiastically.

"My dad is great at catching fish," she tells the nice lady.

"Oh, I have no doubt of that," she responds.

Then they both look at me and wait for my answer.

"I'll have to check the dates, but I would be honored to share what I know," I promise.

"How wonderful!" nice lady exclaims. "I'm so glad you came by this morning."

"Me too," I tell her, and I really mean it. This feels right. This is the feeling I should get when I think about fishing.

Ch 24
The Answer

I take a sip of water from the plastic, Holiday Inn branded cup and slide the curtain open. Across the highway, I spy a giant leaping bass logo. I can't help but wonder if my boss, Greg, knew that I would literally be able to see the Gurnee Mills Bass Pro Shop from the window of my hotel room. The programming conference has been great, but it really has been tough to stay focused on work. It just so happens that this is the week of the store's annual Spring Fishing Classic, complete with huge sales, manufacturers' booths and demonstrations, and a star-studded lineup of fishing pros giving seminars.

I let the curtain fall shut, go to the desk and page through the sales flyer that came in my complementary newspaper yesterday morning. I've probably looked at it 50 times but I still can't believe my eyes.

Seminar Schedule
Saturday 10 am
"Springtime Fishing with Square-Lipped Crankbaits"
Presented by Bass Pro Shops very own Rick Clunn

I know I will not oversleep, but I pull my iPhone from my pocket and set the alarm for 8 am. Suddenly, it occurs to me that Rick Clunn might be in this hotel at this very moment. *Get a grip, William* I laugh to myself. I'm not someone who gets starstruck or nervous about celebrities, but I am pretty anxious to see Clunn in person. I'm uneasy because I've realized that I need to take advantage of this opportunity to answer a few questions rattling around in the back of my mind. For as well as my training is going, I find myself haunted by my brother-in-law's comments. If this mental conditioning works as well as Clunn says, why isn't he dominating every tournament? I believe I'm on the right path. I believe Clunn's ideas will help me take my performance to amazing new levels. But, why doesn't he win every tournament? There must be something I'm missing.

I take another sip of water. I really hope I get the answer tomorrow. I really hope I can think of a way to ask Mr. Clunn without offending him. It's difficult because I have so much respect for the man. I genuinely appreciate how open he has been about his beliefs. I know for a fact that I have already improved my life, but in moments of weakness I'm nagged by doubt.

I've been trying to visualize our meeting and imagine what I might say. *Hey Rick! Remember how you used to be great at fishing?* Every scenario ends with me getting punched in the mouth, and rightly so. Even though I'm apprehensive, I can hardly wait.

* * *

As I walk through the camping section, headed for the giant freshwater aquarium where the seminar will occur, I continue to rehearse the meeting in my head. I'll wait until after he's done speaking before I approach him. I've been to enough of these things to know that the pro always hangs around after his presentation to shake hands, sign autographs, and answer questions. I'll try to wait until the crowd thins a bit so that...good gravy! It's Clunn! As I turn the corner at the end of the aisle, I nearly crash into him.

We make eye contact, and he gives me a polite smile and nod. I try my best to return the gesture. I'm sure I must look like some star-struck goober, but I imagine he's used to that reaction, especially in the aisles of a Bass Pro Shop. For some strange reason, I panic a little and keep walking past him. *I'm not ready yet* I tell myself. *The plan is to talk to him after the seminar. I don't know what to say...* I stop walking. *Alright, William, you know that you will not get a better opportunity than this. Talk to the man!* I turn around and see that Clunn has stopped about half way down the aisle and appears to be studying the specs of a water purifier.

I take a deep breath and try to calm myself. As I approach, it strikes me that he's not nearly as tall as I am. I guess I had pictured him as larger than life. He has a gray, weathered patina from years of exposure to the elements, but a bright spark about him. He carries himself with as much energy and vitality as a man half his age.

"Excuse me...Mr. Clunn," I manage to start. He looks up from the display, puts on a half-smile, and nods politely, just as he had a minute earlier. I'm sensing an unusual mix of supreme confidence and awkward uncomfortableness. I quickly realize that his awkwardness is because of me, or more accurately, for me. He is in perfect control of himself, but approaching fans are always a wildcard.

"I'm a big fan," I tell him. *Ugh! C'mon William, you can do better than that!*

"Thank you," he replies calmly then waits for me to continue.

"I've been reading your Angler's Quest books and I think they're really great." *Okay, that's a little better, but "really great" isn't exactly the insightful kind of feedback I need to launch us into a meaningful conversation.*

"Self awareness is a pretty great topic," he says humbly, as if he neither deserves nor wants to accept praise for his work.

"Absolutely!" I declare perhaps a bit too enthusiastically. He smiles and I continue. "I've been fishing my whole life and competing in tournaments for all of my adult life, but about six months ago it occurred to me that there must be more." He gives me a slow, single nod. Something about his expression changes. Now it seems as though he wants me to continue talking. "I began to research the psychology of high-performance sports and it led me to your Angler's Quest book series. I've got to tell you, the information you've shared has changed my life." I realize that what I just said to him could be perceived as crazy fan gushing, but I said it confidently, sincerely, and with a level head.

He nods in agreement and says, "We all have the power to do great and amazing things. So much of what humans are capable of is often misunderstood and almost always underutilized."

A shiver of goosebumps runs up the back of my neck. Clunn's passion for this information is palpable. Suddenly, I realize that I've used my own power to put myself in this moment–to be standing in the aisles of Bass Pro Shop having a philosophical discussion with *the* Rick Clunn. More goosebumps. "So true," I agree. "Why do you suppose more anglers aren't studying these philosophies?"

He chuckles and shakes his head. "I really don't know." Then he considers it for a moment. "Ego, perhaps? Maybe it has become human nature to be more self-centered than self-aware."

I nod and smile. Suddenly, my stomach knots up because I realize it's time to ask the difficult question. "Mr. Clunn...with all due respect..." He raises one eyebrow suspiciously because we all know that phrase is never followed by anything good. "...and I have a ton of respect for your philosophies. I mean, I am absolutely convinced..." He smiles and shakes his head letting me know that I've established my level of adoration and I should get to my point. "Well...is it possible that people notice you haven't been winning as much lately and assume all of the psychological stuff doesn't really work?" There, I asked it. Now, I brace myself for my well-deserved punch in the mouth.

Clunn looks down and doesn't say anything right away. He rubs the back of his neck, as if to relieve some tension while he contemplates his answer. "No...I don't think that's the issue. I mean, I had an amazing run starting in the mid-1970s lasting more than ten years. Even then, people were hesitant to embrace these ideas."

"Good point," I agree. I'm so glad he's open to discussing this.

"There are two things I'd like to tell you about seeking perfection." Clunn pauses to make sure he has my attention.

I cannot possibly be listening more intently I think to myself. *I wish I was recording this! Alright, focus! Commit this to memory!*

He continues. "You must first understand that to reach peak performance you must forget about reaching the peak. Perfection is in how you climb the mountain. Focusing on the top will not get you there. Instead, focus on using all of your senses to their fullest and being completely aware. Focus on the art of what you're doing rather than the egocentric desire for honors, awards, money and fame. Push yourself beyond what you know your limitations to be. Then it happens..." He makes solid eye contact with me. "The impossible becomes possible and you find yourself standing on the peak."

Coincidentally, someone tests a wind chime two aisles over in the home decor department. The haunting notes fill the air just as he finishes his sentence. *Alright, that was kind of funny but don't you dare smile* I threaten myself.

He continues with 100% conviction. "I can assure you that by living this philosophy it is possible to find perfection."

I nod. I want him to know I am listening but I don't dare speak. He said there were two things he would tell me and I don't want to interrupt his train of thought.

He pauses to make sure I've had enough time to let his words soak in. He clears his throat and continues. "The journey is different for everyone. Be open to the idea that the view from the top may not be what you expected when you started your climb. I don't mean that in a negative way, but you may experience a paradigm shift, a revolution, a metamorphosis. Once you understand how to harness the power of mind, body and spirit working together, you may question how you want to use it."

I nod but wait a moment to speak. When I'm sure he's done, I realize I don't know how to respond. I struggle and finally decide on, "Wow. Thank you." I know that response isn't exactly brilliant, but it's sincere and I think he knows that.

"My pleasure," he assures me. His eyes quickly scan the big store then settle on his wristwatch. "I really could discuss these ideas all day, but right now I have to go sell some crankbaits." He gives me a coy wink and motions in the direction of the audience gathering for his seminar.

"Oh, absolutely," I respond. "Wow. It's been a tremendous pleasure to meet you and I can't thank you enough for sharing your wise words."

With that, he places the water purifier back on the shelf, smiles and nods courteously, and heads toward the big aquarium. I watch him disappear into the growing crowd.

Ch 25
Just Like Old Times

I frame my smiling brother and his oversized bass and click the shutter release. "Let me get one more to be safe," I suggest. "Hold him up a little higher...good...now, try to look smarter."

Doug uses his free hand to show me his middle finger.

I snap another quick picture and we both laugh.

Today has been great on many levels. As a fishing day, it was perfect–perfect weather, perfect scenery and perfect company. As a tournament practice day, it was a huge success–flawless decision making and execution, lots of good-sized fish and a pattern that we were able to replicate in several different areas. And as a day to reconnect with an old friend, it was priceless–lots of laughs, not a single second revisiting past mistakes, and a host of new memories that only a day fishing with an old friend can provide.

Ch 26
Nothing Without Them

"Well, that was absolutely delicious," I assure my beautiful wife, as I lick the last few crumbs from my fingertips.

"Delicious," Dacey echoes.

"I'm so glad you both enjoyed it," Trixie tells us warmly. "I hope you saved a little room for desert," she says, knowing full well that neither my daughter nor I have ever refused desert.

"I'd hate to disappoint you, dear," I confess. She smiles her approval.

"Dacey darling? Will you please help me clear the table?" Our well-trained kiddo slides down from her chair and begins collecting silverware.

"We're going to miss you the next couple days," Trixie tells me sincerely as she stacks our plates. "Are you excited about the tournament?"

"I really am. More than ever," I assure her.

"Good," she approves.

"I guess I'm always excited just before the first tourney of the year, but I'm usually nervous too," I explain. "This year I'm not nervous, I'm eager. I feel like a racehorse in the gate. Let's start this thing. I'm ready to run!" I chuckle at my slightly over-the-top analogy.

"I like the sound of that," she says encouragingly. "I'm still listening, she promises as she heads into the kitchen with the dirty dishes.

I continue slightly louder. "It's hard to explain. On one hand I'm not really concerned with winning, but on the other hand I know that I will win. It's a truly amazing feeling."

Dacey comes back into the dining room with three clean spoons. She smiles at me as she places a spoon at each of our places around the table.

"And actually, maybe "win" isn't even the right word—maybe it's "perform." I know that I will perform at my highest level. When all is said and done, as long as I have done my best, then I will feel like a winner."

Trixie emerges from the kitchen with three bowls of dark-red sliced strawberries topped with a dollop of fresh whipped cream.

"That's a really positive, deeply philosophical way of looking at things, dear," she says as if she's impressed.

"Yeah, I guess I have been giving this a lot of thought lately," I say humbly.

"Well, I'm very impressed by your dedication. I feel like this process has been very good for you—good for all of us, really."

I look at her beautiful smile. I look in her eyes—I mean, really look deep in her eyes. Then I turn my gaze to my little girl, happily devouring a giant spoonful of desert. She smiles at me with her cheeks puffed out like a chipmunk.

"I want to thank you both for allowing me the time and space to pursue my passion. I know I'm very fortunate to have such a supportive family."

"That's what families do, William," Trixie says as she reaches across the table and squeezes my hand. "The truth is," she continues, "it feels like we've spent more quality time together lately than ever before. It's been nice."

"Well you better get used to it, baby," I say sincerely, but in a silly voice.

She giggles and raises her water glass. "Congratulations in advance. I'm sure you'll have a great tournament, but we're proud of you no matter what happens!" she toasts. All three of our glasses meet over the middle of the table. "Clink!"

I take an exaggerated, slurpy sip of my water like it's fine champagne, mostly in a effort to make Dacey giggle. "Thank you, dear," I tell Trixie as I lower my glass. Then I look her in the eye and with 100 percent confidence tell her, "But I am going to win."

Ch 27
Get My Head Right

I step out into the parking lot. It's still dark. I was wide awake an hour before my alarm this morning so I got an early start. The air is still cool and calm. I stretch and take a deep breath, and for a split second I wonder if anyone is arriving at the office where I work right now. That will definitely be the last time I think about work for the next three days.

As I make my way around the boat to unhitch the safety straps, I notice fresh, wet tire tracks from the ramp to the parking area. My eyes follow the tracks to a big, red, extended-cab Tundra, plastered with sponsor stickers, pulling a matching, dual-axle Ranger trailer. *Looks like a pretty new rig,* I think to myself. *Maybe even brand new. I don't recognize him. Must be a pretty heavy hitter. There are always a couple big sticks in these tournaments.* Quickly, I remind myself that the cost of the boat is not necessarily an indication of the fishing skill level of the owner. I'm a bit surprised. I really thought I'd be the first one launching at this hour, but I guess this is the first big tourney of the year. People get pretty excited after the long winters around here. I know I'm one of them.

The eastern sky is just beginning to hint of the dawning day. Time to get this party started. With the red, green and white beacons of my running lights leading the way, I carefully back my tailer down the shadowy ramp.

Today isn't as much about catching fish as it is about making sure my mind is right for tomorrow. In the past, I would probably just go fishing. Furthermore, I would probably end up in a lot of the spots I already knew held fish, because sadly, if the day ended without catching fish, my confidence would be shaken and I would definitely flounder on tournament day. I realize now that it was a ridiculous approach. There is no winner on practice day. My new plan is to spend most of my time today confirming conditions and idling around with my GPS marking the quickest safe routes to the areas I plan to fish, but I will keep an open mind. If a feeling hits me, I may try to locate some secondary fish near my primary spots. Mostly, I want to feel the "flow" of nature. I want to feel a connection. I want to feel confidence in my decisions.

I'm idling to an area just a few minutes downstream from the launch–a little wing dam near shore, well off of the main channel. Because of its proximity to the launch, it's definitely not a secret spot. I don't think this is where I'll start tomorrow. In fact, I probably will not end up fishing this at all tomorrow. I'm picturing this as more of a late in the day, last-minute, backup sort of spot. I'm only heading here today because I've started earlier than expected and think it's wise to wait for safe light before making a full-speed run. Plus, it will give me a chance to warm up a bit and get into that "flow." I take this opportunity as I idle for the next several minutes to meditate and reset my mind. I focus on my breath. The last several months of practice is really paying off, because I'm able to feel completely calm almost instantly.

I pull in just downstream of the riffled water as it flows over the obstruction. The surface disturbance in the current makes it easy to locate the structure even in this low light. Using my trolling motor to hold position, I wait...and I listen...and I observe. I don't even have a fishing rod in my hand. What does this area have to offer? In the distance, I hear the distinct sound of a big two-stroke outboard revving up. Someone else at the launch, no doubt. Quickly, I draw my focus back to the wing dam in front of me. I study the direction of the current. I note the size of the eddy near shore. I look for differences in the intensity of the disturbed surface water, imagining the shape, the high and low spots, the width, the composition of the structure hidden under water. I watch my electronics for depth changes. I look for...

"Splash...splish,splish...splish, SPALOOSH!"

Off in the distance, a good 50 yards off the end of the wing dam, the calm is broken by the obvious sounds of a feeding predator. I freeze and focus all of my attention in that direction. I strain in the morning's early light to watch for clues. It doesn't take long.

"SPLASH. SPLASH...splish, splish...SPLASH!"

I set my trolling motor on high and grab a rod rigged with a chrome and black Chug Bug. *What could be holding feeding fish this far out on the flat, I wonder? Could they be bass? I hope they aren't white bass.* As soon as I'm within range I fire my topwater lure to the spot where I last saw the disturbance. I jerk the rod tip down and the cupped face of my bait chugs and gurgles across the surface. The current washes it a few feet and I pop it again. I wait, then pop it a third time and a violent strike takes down my lure. I lean back on the rod and a good-sized smallmouth heads for the sky. *Holy crap! Nice, nice, nice!* I giggle to myself. *Nice fish!* As I fight the fish, I quickly scan the area for competitor's boats. If anyone is around, I'll try to play it cool, maybe even stop fighting the fish altogether. I'd rather lose him today and have his friends to myself tomorrow. This is an odd, middle-of-nowhere kind of spot. For as many boats as I've seen fishing this wing dam, I've never seen anyone out here. I believe the boat I heard starting a couple minutes ago is headed the other way upriver. *Perfect!*

As the fish gets close to the boat, I play the angles, and at just the right moment I haul up on the rod and use his momentum to swing him in. I notice just as he's coming out of the water that a second smallie is swimming with him, trying to fight him for the bait. The second fish is even bigger than the one I've hooked, but the one I've hooked is a beast! I quickly unhook my catch and lay him on the measuring board. Nineteen and a half inches! *Nice start,* I tell myself. As I slide him back into the river, the splashing starts up again in the same spot. That's all I need to see. I put the rod down. No sense in catching any more from this spot today. However, I'd like to try to figure out what they're doing here. I get back on the trolling motor and turn my focus to my depth finder. I discover that the wing dam actually does stretch all the way out here. Near the shore, the rocky, manmade structure starts 8 feet deep and rises to just 2 feet beneath the surface. Out here the flat is about 10 feet deep and the rocks are only piled 1-1/2 to 2 feet tall—topping out 8 feet beneath the surface. But more than that, my electronics reveal that something has lodged against it in this deeper water. I think it may be a giant log or maybe part of someone's dock, or maybe both that have washed downriver in the early spring and come to rest here. This new current break seems to be a perfect ambush spot for hungry smallmouth bass. While a spot like this probably doesn't last year after year, it can be pure gold for right now. I quickly mark a few waypoints on my GPS and get out of here before someone sees me.

Well that was cool, I congratulate myself. That is exactly how a tournament fisherman hopes a practice day will start. I remind myself that I need to remain open to all possibilities today. Stay focused. Breathe. Listen to what the fish are trying to tell me.

I decide that I should head to the spot that I had assumed would be my starting spot for tomorrow. I'm excited about the possibilities.

Thundering down the river, I spot five likely competitors' boats. I note what they're doing, but I don't worry about them. Today is about me and the fish. Breathe. Focus. Fish.

Now this spot will require a bit of fancy driving to gain access. I'm not talking about anything too dangerous, but a wrong turn will likely leave me on a shallow sandbar. Not a tournament day ender, but it eats precious fishing time to get out and push my boat back to "floatable" water. I checked the predicted river pool levels before I left home and it looks like this cut should be accessible, but it will be close. The channel is narrow and winding. For today, I'm going to idle in and get a good trace on my GPS. Tomorrow morning I'll have one eye on the electronic map while we're flying in at full speed. The faster this 3,000-pound boat is moving, the less water it needs under it to float.

Up ahead I spy the narrow entrance off the main river. The tree-covered points visually overlap each other a bit, forming a tight S-turn, but making the opening virtually invisible from a distance. I've nicknamed it "The Bat Cave."

I ease off of the throttle and the smooth hull settles back into the water a good hundred yards from my destination. Out of habit, I carefully scan the water for other boats. Another boat may cause me to abort my mission rather than point out the location to anyone else. Then I laugh to myself when I realize what I'm doing. I don't want to help my competitors defeat me, but worrying about them to the point of distraction is doing just that. Today I'm making a conscious effort to focus on the fish rather than the field. Slowly, I ease through the opening in the trees and follow the current as it turns hard to the right, then doubles back on itself to the left. I make a mental note of a stump on the inside turn, but I don't think it should be difficult to miss it tomorrow. I'll be favoring the outside of the turn where the deeper water flows.

Once I'm through the curves, the cut widens for several hundred yards. On the right is deeper water–a steep undercut bank littered with deadfall trees and stumps. The left side has a wide expanse of matted weeds and lily pads. This all looks good, and in fact, this area can hold some fish, but the best part is up ahead where it narrows back down and turns hard to the left. The current gets concentrated there and has scoured out a deep spot right on the edge of a huge shallow backwater area. Shallow lily pads stretch almost as far as you can see–hundreds of acres. That edge where the deep current meets the shallow, still water is a natural feeding spot that big bass take advantage of.

I nose my boat into a slack-water spot just before the narrows and turn off the big motor. I feel the hull dragging bottom as it comes to rest in the shallow water near shore. I remove my life vest and step up onto the front deck. Again, I don't reach for a rod. I take a deep breath and simply observe. The leaves in the trees are still. The water appears to be slightly clearer than the main channel. Far off in the distance I hear the familiar sound of an air horn signaling the lock is open to let boats or shipping barges continue on their way. I bring my attention back to this area. I try to imagine the bass lined up on that current edge just ahead of me with their noses sticking just out from under the canopy of pads, waiting for breakfast to wash by. I visualize the cast I'll make. My frog bumps and fumbles its way along–an irresistible target. I smile because I know I'll be battling them tomorrow. This is awesome! I'm incredibly relaxed and comfortable. This is exactly where I'm supposed to be in this moment.

I decide to visualize another cast. My frog lands with a soft "plop," hesitates briefly, then begins to move with the current. In my mind I can see the bass lined up just ahead. They're all nice ones–not giants, but good, solid tournament keepers. Just as my frog moves into position, they all scatter as a beast of a bass comes zooming in from behind my boat, grabs the frog, and returns to the flooded timber on the deeper undercut bank. The image startles me a bit, and I snap back from my meditative state. I laugh nervously and actually say aloud to myself, "Well, that was weird." I look at the area where I imagined the attack. Then I look at the tangle of fallen trees where the big pretend fish had retreated.

Using the trolling motor, I move my boat back into the deeper water and pick up my jig rod. I carefully analyze the first tree as I move closer. I try to imagine how the branches cross each other and form pockets and shady spots. Where would a bass be positioned in this mess? Carefully I pitch my jig to the upstream side of the thickest part of the trunk. I feel the current wash my bait along as it bumps down the tree. I feel the weight of my line pulling against a branch. With my full concentration, I reel my leadhead jig right up to it, and give it a light snap, so it knocks on the branch without coming over it. I wait a second, then repeat the knock. I pop it once more, then let the lure free fall back down to the bottom. Instead of the sensation of the lure landing on the silty bottom, I feel a sharp tick. Instinctively, I reel the slack out quickly and set the hook hard. Initially, there is no movement and I worry that I may have just lost a $4 jig to a deep snag. Then I feel a powerful head shake and my line heads away from the tree. I change the angle of the rod and follow the direction of my line, preparing for a fight. Apparently, the fish was preparing itself too. The battle is longer and more spirited than a typical largemouth fight. Twice he runs under the boat, and even jumps on the other side behind me. I reach for his bottom jaw and haul every bit of 5 pounds of healthy largemouth into the boat.

Well isn't that interesting? I ask myself. Looking down the shoreline at several more tangles of wood in the water, I hold the fish up and ask him, "So, do you have any friends down there or are you guarding this shoreline for yourself?" I slip the big beast back into the water and consider my options. I've been burned in practice before. A big rogue, fluke of a fish can really screw up a

166

solid plan. With the trolling motor on high, I zip ahead 40 or 50 yards, passing several good-looking targets without a cast. I pull up to the next tree and ease a cast in along the upstream side of the trunk. Almost immediately I get a tick. This time, rather than setting the hook, I apply gentle, steady pressure and try to lead the fish away from cover in hopes to get a look at him without hooking him. Even without loading the rod up, it feels like a pretty solid fish. Almost according to plan, he doesn't open his mouth until he's right at the side of my boat and within a foot of the surface. I get a good look at the white flash of his belly as he turns. Nice fish–at least 3, maybe 4 pounds!

I get back on the trolling motor and cruise all the way to the far end of this bank, to the first logs I noticed on my way in. This time it takes three whole casts before I get a bite. Once again, I'm able to get a good look and once again it's a good fish. I gently shake the rod tip until he releases my jig and returns to his tangled hideout.

"I'll see you tomorrow, my fat little friends," I call out. "Stay hungry," I remind them then laugh like an evil genius. "Bwa ha ha!"

* * *

The desolate launch I left before light today is now a beehive of activity. There are several boats, mostly bass boats, in various stages of leaving the water. Some are tied to the pier, some are idling around, waiting for a partner to back the trailer down the ramp, and some are on their trailers headed up the ramp to the parking lot. I notice a sandy spot on shore off to the right side of the ramp. I ease the nose up until the hull is grounded and shut down the big motor. I want to take a minute to reflect on the amazing day I just had, but my sense of common courtesy tells me I should get my boat out of the way as quickly as possible. There are a lot of boats moving through this area right now. Everyone wants to get back to their hotel rooms, get the boat batteries charging, shower up, and head to the pre-tournament meeting.

I dig through the glovebox, locate the truck keys, and tuck them safely in my front jean pocket. As I hop from the nose of the boat to shore, I'm greeted by old Carl Marquette. "Hey, William. You leave any for me out there?" he kids–pretty standard fisherman small talk.

"Oh, I've got a feeling you don't need my fish," I kid back.

He laughs as he hustles off to his boat tied to the dock. "We'll see how it goes," he calls. "Good luck tomorrow, William."

"Thanks Carl. Same to you." I begin to walk across the grass toward the parking lot. Along the way, I chat briefly with several people I've seen at these tournaments for years. "Hey, how's it going?" "There he is." What's the word, Champ?" "See you at the meeting."

Once I get the truck in line for my turn at the launch ramp, I realize I'll have several minutes to kill. I turn the radio down, breathe a few times and begin to recount the day's events. Without ever throwing a cast at any of the spots Doug and I located last weekend, I caught a huge bag of fish. In fact, I never made a second cast anywhere I caught a fish today. If this were the weigh-in I'd have pretty close to 20 pounds. I wouldn't say the fishing was easy, but my attitude, my confidence and my execution were perfect. I let the fish tell me where they were and what they wanted. I was at once relaxed and hyper-aware, and everything just felt natural and intuitive. That was a great day of fishing. I feel incredibly fortunate to have spent today doing what I was doing.

* * *

"William Buckner. Dale Cole. Boat 16," the tournament director announces over the crowd of competitors.

Sixteen. Not bad in a field of 130 boats, I think to myself as I weave my way to the predetermined meeting spot in front of the Ranger sponsor boat.

"Sixteen," a tall, young man in a blue Yamaha T-shirt calls out.

"Sixteen," I respond. "You must be Dale." I extend my hand and he shakes it enthusiastically.

168

"Yep, Dale. I'm sorry, I didn't catch your name," he tells me earnestly.

"William. William Buckner."

"William, he repeats and smiles. "Okay if I call you Bill?"

"No, I go by William," I tell him in a friendly way that lets him know it's not negotiable.

"Fair enough. William it is." He nods and smiles.

"Good. Now, step into my office, Dale," I kid, indicating a spot in the parking lot away from the masses.

When we're finally in a reasonably private area, I begin the standard tournament pairing conversation.

"So, where are you from, Dale?"

"I live up in Duluth."

"Oh, Duluth? I've spent some time up in that area," I share. "My college roommate was from Duluth, and we'd go back up there hunting and fishing. Great area for anything outdoors."

"Yeah, I just finished school there last year, and I haven't left yet. Actually, I grew up in Ely."

"Oh, way up north," I say.

"Yeah, nothing but outdoor activities up there."

"True," I agree. "So have you fished the river down here very much?"

"First time," he admits. "Just got into town last night. We fished today, but that's all I've ever seen of this water."

"Really? So how'd you end up in this tourney?"

"I agreed to sign up as a guaranteed co-angler to help out a buddy. That's who I fished with today."

"I see. Well this is one of my favorite places to fish in the whole state. I think we'll have a pretty good day tomorrow."

His face brightens a bit. "Excellent. So what kind of stuff should I be prepared for?"

"Honestly, a little bit of everything. I mean, typical stuff, nothing fancy. Topwater early, maybe some froggin', possibly some mat punching, probably pitching jigs on wood. Seriously, pretty standard stuff."

"Okay. Would five rods be too many?"

"Fine with me. There should be plenty of room for you." I briefly consider telling him about my day today, and even my new psychological approach, but I couldn't see a good reason to. I know I'm excited about it. In fact, I know it's the reason I'll win tomorrow. But I've learned the hard way that not everyone understands or appreciates it right away. My position at this point is that I'm glad to share what I know if someone asks, but otherwise I'll just keep it to myself.

We exchange contact info and plan to meet at the front corner of the parking lot at 4:45. With that we shake hands and part ways. *Seems like a nice enough guy,* I think to myself. He's exactly the kind of draw you want when you're on a ton of biting fish. He seems experienced enough that he shouldn't be constantly snagged, and will probably be focused on his own fishing. Plus, his lack of experience on this body of water means he won't spend the day telling me about all the spots he caught one once.

The partner draw was the only thing I was worried about at all. I wish it was time to launch right now. I can't wait to go fishing!

* * *

My room is dark. I lay on my back and run through my checklist one more time. Gas tank topped off. Batteries are charging, in fact, nearly charged last time I checked. New line on every rod I plan to fish tomorrow. Hooks sharpened. Everything packed up and waiting by my motel room door. iPhone alarm set. Backup motel clock/radio alarm set. Weather checked. It looks like there is a weak front moving in tonight. Cooler tomorrow morning with a bit of wind, but warming nicely in the afternoon. Overall a pleasant day is predicted.

I smile and remind myself of how grateful I am to be here doing what I love. I'm not anxious at all. The butterflies that normally keep me awake the night before a big tournament are gone. I'm comfortable. Of all the places in the world, I know that I'm supposed to be right here. Tomorrow is my day.

Ch 28
Remember To Breathe

I awake refreshed, 10 minutes ahead of schedule. I take advantage of this time by visualizing my coming day. I know where the fish are. I know when it's time to make a change. I execute flawlessly. I raise the first place trophy over my head. I accept the accolades humbly. Then my alarm clock lets me know it's time to live it.

There is a noticeable chill in the air as I roll through town toward the launch ramp. Even though it's early, I'm not the only rig on the road. Like I said, everyone is excited at the first tournament of the year.

At 4:42 I round the corner into the parking lot and pull over at the predetermined meeting spot. There are several co-anglers lined up– life vest slung over one shoulder, struggling to hold too many rods in one hand, most transporting more tackle than I have in my whole boat–but no Dale. Not a big deal, I think to myself. I am a couple minutes early. I hop out of my truck and get the boat ready for our big day. Safety straps removed. Drain plug in. Running lights on. Okay, still no Dale. I pull my iPhone out of my pocket. 4:47. I watch other boats pull in, meet their partners and head to the launch. We still have plenty of time, but I really like to launch early. I've never had a partner that completely flaked out on me, like overslept or some-thing like that. I can't help but wonder what would happen if this is my first. I check the time again. 4:54. I find his phone number and give him a call.

"Hello?" says Dale.

"Hey Dale, it's William. Just wanted to see where you are."

"Oh. My buddy needed to stop off at the gas station. We should be there in two minutes," he promises casually.

"Okay. Cool. Just wanted to make sure. See you soon."

"Okay. See ya."

Not terrible, I remind myself. I know sometimes it's tricky when you're at the mercy of someone else driving. Still, I can remember when I was a co-angler. I absolutely never left my ride for the day waiting or wondering where I was. I would be there early. In fact, even as the boater, I've never made the co-angler wait. It just seems like common courtesy. Here's a guy I don't know. We've made a plan to spend the whole day together on a boat and we've both invested a lot of time and money to be here. Why would we want to start the day like this?

I circle the boat, trying to find tasks to pass the time. I take my life vest out of the storage compartment and put it in the driver's seat. I dig into the cooler, find a small bottle of orange juice and gulp it down. I look at my phone again. 5:05. In front of me I see a line of red trailer lights stretching from the ramp all the way back to the parking lot entrance. I realize my jaw is clenched and my thoughts are dark. I remember to breathe and remind myself that this is my day. The current whereabouts of my partner means nothing. Relax.

At 5:10 a white F-150 followed by a yellow Skeeter pulls up next to me and Dale hops out.

"Morning, William," he says like there's nothing wrong.

I quickly decide there is no good that can come from confronting him on his tardiness. Focus on the fish. "Hey, Dale. I've got the compartment behind your seat all cleared out for you. Do you need help carrying anything?"

"Cool. No, I think I've got it, thanks."

I take the opportunity for one last lap around the boat to make sure I haven't forgotten anything. As I come around the back corner to inspect the prop, a truck pulls up behind me. It's headlights illuminate my outboard. When I'm satisfied everything is okay, I turn my attention away from the prop. I look above the glare of the lights and spot the driver of the vehicle. Our eyes lock. Cam. Cam Seavers. I've been so focused on my fishing I hadn't even considered the possibility that he would be fishing today. I haven't seen him or spoken to him since his little blow up. I smile sheepishly and give him the old head nod/single flick of the wrist wave. His only response is to continue staring daggers at me. Alright, I think to myself. If that's how he wants to play it, that's his problem. At least I was a big enough man to be cordial.

"Ready when you are, William," Dale calls.

"Let's hit it," I respond and head toward my truck. When I open the driver's door I look back over my shoulder at Cam. He hasn't budged. Same spot, same crazy death stare. I shake my head just enough that I know he can see it, then climb in and shut the door.

* * *

Boat 15," the tournament director calls over the P.A.

"Here we go," I alert my partner as I guide my boat into position behind Boat 15.

Boat 16," he announces.

I wave my hand over my head to get his attention.

"Thank you, Boat 16. 2:30 check in time....Boat 17."

I sit up straight and push my yellow-lens sunglasses tight against my face. I look over each shoulder to confirm the position of the boats around me as I idle the last several yards to the main channel buoy. The boat ahead of us guns it and hops up on pad. I look at my co-angler and extend a hand. "Good luck today, Dale."

"You too," he responds and gives my hand a solid shake.

As I clear the marker, I put the gas to the floor. The big motor roars to life as the hull leaps out of the water. We're early enough in the launch order that the water ahead of us isn't quite as rough as it will be for boat 130. I still need to pay attention to the wakes criss-crossing ahead of me but it should be a fairly smooth ride. Actually, we're just going to make a short run to our first spot. When I heard our early launch number, I decided that I would start on those big smallies I found off the end of the wing dam yesterday. The spot is coming up quickly at this speed, so I begin to edge over to the left side of the channel, but so is Boat 15. As we get nearer, it's obvious that he's heading for the wing dam, but worse, there are already two other boats on it. And, of course, one of them is already fishing the deeper spot I found. I look over my right shoulder, put the gas back down to the floor and ease my way back over to the right. *Well, I knew that was a community spot,* I remind myself. *I guess I shouldn't be too surprised. Those fish have probably been feeding and giving away their location to everyone who checked that wing dam.*

At this point, there are only a few rooster tails on the horizon ahead of me. I need to stay alert while driving at speed, but I try to breathe and relax. I search to feel that connection. I remind myself that this is my day. I smile because I really can't think of anywhere I'd rather be right now.

After about a 10-minute run, I spot the "Bat Cave" just ahead. There are no boats ahead of me and it's about a quarter-mile back to the next boat behind me.

"Hang on," I ready my partner as I turn toward the narrow entrance in the shoreline.

We shoot between the points, cut hard left, then hairpin nearly 180 degrees to the right. The main channel disappears from view behind us. I ease off of the throttle and the boat settles into the slightly deeper water. It feels like we've gone through some portal to a different dimension far from the excitement of the tournament. Everything here seems natural and undisturbed. Although it can't be true, it's easy to imagine we're the first humans to lay eyes on this spot.

"Wow, this stretch sure looks bass-y," my partner confirms.

"Good area," I assure him as I idle toward the sweet spot where it narrows back down. Just shy of our destination, I shut off the big motor and hop to the front deck.

"Good morning, ladies," I call out playfully to the bass. It feels so great to finally be here after training for it all winter. *Have fun,* I remind myself, *but stay focused.* I draw a deep, cleansing breath and prepare myself for the first cast, just like I've done a million times before. Nice and easy. I pick up my trusty frog rod. I exhale slowly, load the rod over my shoulder and let a perfect cast fly toward the edge of the pads. My lure lands with a soft plop, hesitates briefly, then begins to glide with the current. I point my rod tip down and begin a series of sharp twitches, causing the frog to sashay side-to-side in a zig-zag pattern along the front edge of the vegetation. Just before the end of my lure's route I see the water boil under the next lily pad. I brace myself for the inevitable attack...and nothing happens. I let the frog sit motionless, then give it a couple more twitches. Nothing. I reel in quickly and place the next cast a few feet further into the pads and repeat the dance. Nothing. My third cast is a couple feet further in. This time when the frog reaches the edge of the pads the water explodes violently. "That's more like it," I celebrate. "I knew they were...ugh, pike."

Dale arrives at my side with the net. He senses my disappointment. "Pike," I repeat.

"Pike?" he echoes. "Well, I guess you've got to get them out of the way. You know we caught quite a few northerns yesterday, but we caught bass mixed right with them," he consoles.

"Oh yeah. I'm not worried yet," I tell him with my best attempt at a chuckle. I swing the small, snaky beast in and gingerly remove my frog from his mouth, careful not to tear it on his plethora of pointy teeth. After rinsing the stinky slime from my hand, I take a deep breath and picture my next cast.

"Net! Net!" Dale calls from the back deck.

I set my frog rod at my feet, pivot, grab the net and leap to the back deck in one, smooth, cat-like move. I can see from the amount of pressure this fish requires that Dale's got a pretty good one on. "Nice and easy," I coach.

After a handful of attempts to escape, the fish surrenders by the boat and I scoop him with the net.

"Yes!" Dale exclaims with an enthusiastic fist pump.

I hand him the net, stretched by a healthy bass with a 6-inch purple worm hanging from its lip, and head back to the front deck. "Nice start," I tell him. "Probably just over 3 pounds."

"Nice is right. Thanks, William!"

Once again, I grab my trusty frog rod and prepare my cast. *Where did he even catch that fish*, I ask myself. *It must have been from that first lay-down log. I would prefer if he wouldn't fish those yet, but I guess he really doesn't have a great shot at the pads.* This is definitely one of the tricky things about having two guys fishing out of the same boat, but each man for himself. *When I'm practicing alone, I can manage an area however I see fit. The way this spot is shaped makes it difficult to hold the boat so he can't fish ahead of me. I plan to go back and fish the logs, but I wanted to start with these pads. Alright, wait. It doesn't matter what he's doing. Breathe. Focus. Fish.* I inhale deeply and raise my rod over my shoulder.

"Net! Net! Net!" comes the cry from the back of the boat.

I gladly respond with the net, but catch the voice in my head saying, *Purple worm? Seriously?*

"I think it's a pretty good one," he tells me.

The fish rolls near the boat and I scoop it cleanly with the landing net. He's right. It is a pretty good one–a little smaller than his first fish, maybe 2-3/4.

"Nice job, Dale," I compliment him sincerely.

"Thanks," he responds, half out of breath. "Man, that's a great start," he tells me what I already know.

Fool me twice, I think to myself as I reposition the boat to work down the shoreline of flooded timber.

"Looks like they're on this bank this morning," I say matter-of-factly, like I expected this possibility. It's true. I was planning to fish this, I just thought we'd start on that weed edge and let the sun come up a bit before we hit the shady spots in these tangled logs.

I pick up my jig rod and focus on a few breaths while I study my first target. I smell the sweet, musky air of early morning river. I visualize the bass hiding in the submerged branches. I find the connection with my surroundings and let a soft underhand pitch send my lure off to work.

Ten minutes later and nearly half-way down the bank we've yet to have another bite. I try to decide if there's any chance I have a 6-inch purple worm in my tackle compartment. I don't have anything against the lure. I've certainly caught dozens, if not hundreds, of fish on a purple plastic worm early on in my fishing career. So has practically everyone I know. It's just that you learn new techniques over time and the worm you started with just seems less...I don't know...sophisticated? Refined? I think to myself how funny that logic is. Then I realize how ridiculous it is that I'm spending my time worrying about it. Purple worm is unlikely to be the only thing the fish will eat today. *Remain focused on what's important, William,* I remind myself. *Just breathe and...*

I feel the familiar "tick" on my line as my jig pulls up over a limb, then free-falls into the shadows next to the log. Almost reflexively, I set the hook hard and feel a heavy head shake on the end of my line. That's more like it!

"Net! Net!" I alert my partner. The heavy fish swims like a shot away from the tree. *Well, that helps,* I think to myself, glad that he isn't tangled on a deep branch.

"Get ready, Dale," I direct as I feel my prize coming toward the boat. "There he is, Dale! There he...sheepshead. Damn sheepshead," I announce deflated. That's one thing about fishing the river–you never know what you might catch. Sheepshead, otherwise known as freshwater drum, are fairly common and readily hit most bass fishing presentations. They'll really break your heart on a tournament day.

"You want me to net him anyway?" Dale asks. "I'd hate for that thing to break your line and have you lose a jig."

"Yeah. Go ahead. Net him."

"That's a big one," Dale tries to make the most of the excitement. "Those things will get your heart pumping," he adds as he returns to the back deck.

Unceremoniously, I retract my hook from the big fish's lip. I'll bet he's over 6 pounds. I really thought I had a nice bass. I slide him over the gunnel and exhale with disgust. Standing on the front deck I complete a series of neck stretches in an effort to stay loose. I remind myself to relax and focus, but it has already become a challenge.

We fish the next several hours without another bite.

* * *

I take my hat off and run a hand through my sweaty hair. The sun has been hot for a while now. The fishing has been less than hot. I've tried everything

I can think of–shallow, deep, fast, slow, wood, grass, rocks, main river, backwater. It's been a tough day. I wonder if it has been this tough on everybody.

The clock on my GPS shows we have 2 hours until checkin time–1 hour and 45 minutes with travel time. I remind myself that there's still plenty of time to catch five fish, but I'm having a tough time believing anything I tell myself right now. I know the clock is ticking loudly at this point, but I make the decision to take a break and regroup.

In an effort to give my co-angler a reasonable shot at a fish, I position the boat along a nice weed edge with plenty of targets to throw at.

"I'm gonna take a break for a minute," I inform him. "Think you'll be alright working this over?"

"Sure. Looks as good as anything else," he replies.

I grab a water from the cooler and have a seat on the back edge of the front deck. After a big gulp, I splash some on the back of my neck. My eyes close and I sit up straight, but relaxed. After several deep, cleansing breaths, I go into my meditation ritual. I pay close attention to the way I feel as I inhale deeply. I really need to hurry. There's not much time. *Hurry up and relax!* I laugh to myself and bring my focus back to my breathing. I listen to the sounds around me. My partner fires his spinnerbait out over the weeds and it lands with a familiar "jingle." A red-winged blackbird calls. A small stick lightly drags across the bottom of the hull as we drift along. I can picture myself standing with one foot on the trolling motor pedal. The sun is hot on my shoulders. I can see my target. The bass are lined up along the edge of the pads, just waiting for an easy meal to wander too close. My cast lands perfectly without a splash. As the current begins to wash it along, I bring the frog to life with a well-practiced series of twitches. Two wakes approach from opposite directions and my lure disappears in a violent topwater strike. I set the hook hard and before I know it, a beautiful oversized bass comes swinging aboard. When I open the livewell, I'm thrilled to see four fish even bigger than the one I'm adding. *That's got to put me over 20 pounds,* I think to myself contently. The day is mine.

I open my eyes and know that everything is exactly as it should be.

"I've got an idea," I inform my partner. "I think we're going to switch spots."

"Sounds good to me," he says as he reels in quickly and secures his tackle.

* * *

As I begin to ease over to the left side of the main river channel, I see a boat coming out of the "Bat Cave." But for some reason, I'm not disturbed at all. I'm still going in. I just know this is where the fish are.

As the other boat passes by I offer the standard courteous wave. Then I recognize the driver as Cam Seavers. I had forgotten what his new boat looked like. Apparently, he recognizes me because instead of a return wave he just glares. For a split-second I wonder if we should really fish water behind one of the winning-est fishermen I know. Too late. We shoot between the points, turn left, then double back right as the rest of the world, including Cam, disappears behind us. It's time to catch some fish.

Just as I had done first thing this morning, I ease the boat in just shy of the necked-down channel, about a cast from the edge of the pads.

"I was hoping we'd end up back here," Dale announces.

I smile. I figured he'd been thinking about the spot where he caught his two keepers this morning.

From my spot on the front deck, I gather my focus. Behind me, I hear Dale casting back to the logs that had payed off for him earlier. I sincerely wish him well, but I fight to train my attention back on my own cast.

182

The sun is bright and hot. Everything looks much different than it had in the low early morning light. I study the large black-and-yellow frog swinging from the tip of my heavy-action rod and decide I should make a small adjustment in my presentation. I dig into my tackle compartment and find a smaller-profile white frog. In general, I don't place a lot of stock in colors, keeping my selections simple. In this case, I can feel in my gut that this is a good call. Using a sturdy palomar knot to secure my braid to the nose of my bait, and quickly running a small file along the edge of the hook points, I've given myself every chance to succeed.

"There he is. Net! Net!" my partner calls out.

With cat-like grace, I collect the net and join him on the back deck. He's using fairly stout tackle, so he's able to subdue this fish quickly. In fact, his adrenaline causes him to swing the fish right over the net and onto the deck at this feet. Instinctively, I follow the fish through the air with the net just under it in case the hook pops free.

"Yes!" he celebrates. "About time!"

"Nicely done, Dale!" I pat him hard on the shoulder and head back toward my spot on the front deck.

I knew they were here, I tell myself confidently. One more deep breath. Focus. Fish. I fix my eyes and focus deeply on the weed edge ahead of me, but something isn't right. The water is muddied, really muddied, like caffè latte. *What is this? What could this mean?* My mind races to provide a reasonable answer. In addition to mud, there are bits of shredded stem and stalks, swirling and flowing in the current. I can see a path the width of a boat cut through the bright-green pads. *I know it gets shallow pretty quick under those pads. It would be hard, dirty work to get a bass boat through there. I guess you might force your way in if you had a fish wrapped around some pad stems.* Then I remember seeing Cam on his way out of here. Ugh! *I know he didn't intentionally ruin my spot, but it just figures it would be him. It doesn't matter,* I remind myself, feeling the potential for a complete meltdown weighing heavy on my mind. *I need to fish in the moment, and at this moment I need to change my plan.* I try to think of another spot with this perfect combination of deep water, medium current and pads.

Before I even begin to think, Dale calls for the net. This one is his best of the day at about 3-1/2 pounds. Best I can figure, his four fish will go about 10 pounds. There's still plenty of time for him to fill his limit, but he's already looking pretty good for the co-angler side. He's pretty fired up...and honestly, so am I.

I return to my half of the boat. I look out over the expansive green flat and the cloudy, muddy water. I'm trying not to think too much about Dale's catch, but is that a mistake? Am I focusing so much that I'm not listening to what the fish are telling me? The conditions do make the shady spots in the tangled branches a strong choice. All four of the fish in my boat today were on this shoreline. I struggle to find that confident feeling. Stop, William. Breathe. Focus. Fish.

"I think we should work our way down this deeper bank," I announce to my partner.

"Sounds good to me," he readily agrees, knowing that's where all of his fish have been caught.

I pick up my jig rod, but it doesn't feel right. I can't explain it, but I know it isn't right. Inspired by Dale's plastic worm, I opt for a Texas-rigged plastic. I pick up a creature bait, a Sweet Beaver, in a natural tan-and-brown combination. I'm fairly certain Reaction Innovations, the company that produces the bait, has named it after some sexual innuendo that would make a sailor blush, but no time to think about that now. I line the boat up a short cast from the first logjam. With laser-like focus I analyze the many spots my cast might target. Whenever possible, I like to put my first cast in the highest-percentage spot on a piece of cover. I feel that the element of surprise is more likely to draw a reaction strike, even from fish that aren't actively feeding. The main log in this cluster still has its root system attached, creating a perfect current break

184

and ambush spot for a hungry bass to wait for lunch. Without a ripple, my bait slides into the water along the upstream side of the cover. I feel the bait touch bottom and bounce down the length of the trunk. Then...tick. Without hesitation, I crack the rod back over my shoulder, like a giant springing mouse trap.

"Got him! Net, net, net!"

Unless he's got me wrapped around a branch down there, this feels like a pretty good one. I get my answer quickly as he rolls at the surface. It's a big fish. Dale is quickly ready with the net, but this fish isn't ready. He dives under the boat and just bulldogs me. I can feel his powerful head shake from side to side as he works to expel my bait. I'm eager to get him in the boat, but I remain calm. *Just like you've been practicing,* I remind myself. Eventually he surrenders to the steady pressure and rolls to his side on the surface.

Dale scoops him smoothly and let's out a triumphant "Wooo!"

"Nice work! Thanks partner!" I join the celebration.

"God, that's a beast," he assures me. "You can make up for lost time in a hurry at that pace!"

"That's the plan," I tell him with a smile.

* * *

I bang the livewell lid shut. This is amazing! I have caught four giants in the past hour. They're big enough that I haven't been weighing them, but my best guess would be a 5-1/2, a 5, and two 4-pounders–18 something for four fish. Amazing! Plus, Dale filled his limit with another nice one, probably pushing 4 pounds.

I check the clock on the GPS. Leaving enough time to run to check-in, we've got about 10 minutes to fish. I look ahead up the bank we've been working and realize that there is no more cover in the water. We've meticulously worked every log and branch on this shoreline. Should I turn around and re-work this shore until the clock runs out? I only need one more fish.

As rushed as I am for time, I can't rush this. I search for my concentration and my confidence. Then among all the other sounds of nature, I zero in on the distinct splashing sound of a feeding bass at the far end of the cut, right where it necks down in front of the pads.

Without hesitation, I pick up my frog rod and kick my MinnKota 101 into high gear.

"Hang on, Dale," I warn him half a second too late, as he stumbles to keep his balance.

As we approach, I can see that all of the muddiness has been washed clean by the current. Nature has reset itself, and this little circle of life is back in full swing.

This is my time. Everything is happening exactly as it's supposed to happen. I breathe deep and send my lure out to the pad edge.

My cast lands softly, about 3 feet into the expanse of vegetation. I let it sit motionless with its long strand legs hanging over the edge of a pad. When everything feels "right," I twitch the rod tip, causing my lure to bumble and gurgle it's way to the next pad. I pause briefly, then twitch it again. Pause. Twitch. Pause. Twitch. Suddenly, two significant wakes are surging toward my helpless bait from opposite directions. I give it one more twitch and SSSSLLURP! The white frog disappears. It takes every bit of my concentration to wait motionless until I'm sure he's got it in his mouth. Then I lay back into the long rod and reel for all I'm worth to get the bass headed out of the tough pad stalks and toward the boat.

"Got him! Net! Good one! Net!" My partner is at my side in a flash. He probably heard that strike and knew exactly what was going on.

"Nice fish, William! Get him anywhere near me and he's in the net for sure," he promises.

The fish jumps near the boat, and true to his word, Dale scoops him in mid-air. He holds the net in front of me and I dig in for my prize. When I get my thumb on his lip and raise him up, it occurs to me just how big this fish is.

"Wow! Nice, nice, nice!" Dale tells me. "That's over 4, isn't it?"

"I think it might be," I agree. "Beautiful job with the net, Dale. Thanks!"

"No problem, William."

Time is short, but we both stand silent and motionless, neither of us sure that the last hour could be real.

Finally, Dale breaks the silence. "Holy crap, dude." We make eye contact and share that astonished, relieved, confused sort of laughter. "Holy crap," he repeats. "That's the biggest bag I've ever seen anyone catch in a tournament."

I nod. "Me too." We both laugh again.

I look at the beautiful fish in my hand and then look back at the spot where I caught him. I think about the second wake, but then I look at the clock.

"We should probably call it a day," I tell my partner.

"Absolutely! Let's go weigh these freaks!"

When I open the livewell, I'm thrilled to see four fish bigger than the one I'm adding. *That's got to put me well over twenty pounds,* I think to myself contently. I lower the fish into the well and the water erupts as the big fish fight for position. While I know that it's unlikely, it's not impossible for someone to weigh in a heavier bag. I pause and think about it for a second. Nope. Today is mine.

Ch 29
Justice

The check-in boat, a fully loaded, brand-new Ranger flying a large American flag, is anchored just outside of the launch ramp. I fall in line behind the other tournament boats passing single-file just alongside of the big Ranger. Two tournament officials are onboard, one with a clipboard and the other holding a landing net. Their job is to make sure the competitors are back before the official time is up.

As our turn approaches, Clipboard makes eye contact with me and calls out, "Boat number?"

"16," I call back.

"16? One six?" he confirms as he makes a mark on his clipboard.

I nod and give him a thumbs up.

Then Net reaches out with his net and holds it in front of Dale, who deposits the Number 16 tag that was assigned to us before takeoff this morning.

It's usually about this time that I'm dreading any follow-up questions. Normally, I'd have my hard-luck story well prepared. The voice in my head would typically spend the last hour or two of the competition practicing my excuses. Honestly, I'm not sure how I'll respond today. I'm eager to find out. It's not that I'm excited to brag about myself, I just know pulling through check-in today feels a hell of a lot better than I can remember in the past.

Just when I think I'm not going to get a chance to find out, Net asks, "You guys get 'em today?"

I can't help but smile. "We got 'em pretty good," I tell him. "It was a good day." My partner nods in agreement.

I see that my humble, but confident, answer gets the attention of Clipboard. He shoots us a quick thumbs up, then turns his attention to the next boat behind us.

Dale leans in and extends his hand in a fist. I gladly give him the knuckle bump he's asking for.

Even though we're back early with the first flight of boats, the launch cove is a beehive of activity. We've been given the option of trailering the boat before we weigh in, but with the number and size of fish we have in the well I want to get them weighed as soon as possible. The livewell generally does a good job aerating the water, but I don't want to take any chances. I find an open spot in a long row of boats pulled onto the sandy shore and make my approach. There's a soft scratching sound on the bottom of the hull as the boat grinds to a halt on the beach.

"I'll go grab us a couple bags," Dale offers excitedly as he scrambles over the bow and onto the shore.

"Cool. That's fine with me. I'll start getting the boat organized and packed."

Dale disappears into the crowd and I grab a seat on the back edge of my front deck. *So this is what it feels like to actually look forward to weigh-in,* I think to myself. I take a deep breath and try to memorize everything I'm feeling and seeing and hearing. This really does feel great! In the boat next to me they're loading their catch into the plastic weigh bags. So far they've just been sacking up pretty typical 2-pounders. Good for them, I think sincerely. I've had plenty of days when I would be happy to weigh in any limit. Then I notice further down the line, about 10 boats over, is Cam and his partner for the day. Cam lifts an absolute giant out of the well and slides it into the bag his co-angler is holding open for him. *Good gravy! That fish looked bigger than anything I caught today!,* I lament to myself. *Well, I guess I should have expected that he...*

well, that's weird. I can't hear what they're saying from this distance, but I can see that Cam's partner looks concerned. As he hands the bulging bag to Cam, he says something that causes quite a reaction. Cam looks furious. He quickly looks over both shoulders, then gets right in the guy's face. He tells him something very serious and even pokes the guy in the chest with his finger to emphasize his point. His partner backs down, defeated, then nods like a little kid in trouble. *Yikes! That was uncomfortable. Sure glad I'm not fishing with that nut. Only Cam could catch a huge bag like that and still find something to be upset about.*

But that's his problem, I tell myself. I want to focus on feeling good. I must admit that I'm not quite as confident that I've won, but I still like my chances. I didn't see the rest of his catch. Maybe that was his only good one. It doesn't matter, I remind myself. *I had an amazing day and great results. I was able to defeat my demons time and time again today. Any one of at least a dozen moments I persevered today would have derailed me last year. I only got five bites today, but they were definitely the five I wanted. That was an amazing confirmation that my new course of study is worth pursuing.* I'm thrilled.

The boat rocks as Dale climbs back aboard with two weigh in bags.

"Let's do this thing!" he says excitedly.

* * *

The tips of my fingers are purple from the canvas straps of the heavy weigh bag cutting off the circulation...and it feels great!

As I struggle to transport my catch to the scale, everything about this feels great–the double takes from strangers, the accolades from friends, and the satisfaction of knowing I performed at my highest potential.

As we approach the back of the waiting line, I notice Cam and his partner off to the side behind the stage with their bags of fish. I don't want to think about Cam, but I can't help noticing. He's right in his partner's face again.

Apparently, their heated discussion is not over yet. I imagine the co-angler dared to cast in one of his secret spots and caught one of Cam's fish. I'm so thankful I got him out of my life when I did. Now, back to my day.

"I guess I don't need to measure any of these," the tournament official says with a smile as he pours my fish into the utility sink they use as a measuring and staging station. "Nice job," he tells me as he returns the bag of fish, sans water.

"Boat 16. William Buckner from Chippewa Falls," the director announces from his place on the stage.

I hop up the stairs and join him at the scale.

"Looks like William's got himself a SACK today, folks," he tells the smallish crowd gathered in front of the stage.

The fish flop and squirm in their bag as I anxiously watch the digital readout on the scale flicker between numbers. So far I haven't seen it read anything under 20 pounds. After what seems like a solid five minutes, but is actually less than 10 seconds, the fish hold still and my official weight is announced.

"22 pounds, 3 ounces! That's gonna put William way out in front with the early lead!"

There's a smattering of applause from the audience, but I really can't hear it. I smile reflexively, but I'm in shock. I can't believe what just happened. My knees are weak and I'm sweaty.

"Let's get a weight on that big one," he suggests. Before I know what's happening he tells me that fish goes 5 pounds, 7 ounces, and I'm in the lead for big bass too.

"William, there are still a lot of fishermen left to weigh in. Do you think that weight can hold up?" he asks, then shoves the mic in my face.

"Did you say twenty-two, three?" I ask in a shaky voice.

He laughs playfully. "That's right," he assures me. "So what did you catch them on today?"

"Wow...umm, I mean...flipping a creature bait. Oh, and a frog."

"Well, excellent job, William! Thanks for fishing with us today. Hey, folks. How about another round of applause for our current leader?"

I shake his hand and give a small wave to the crowd as I head off the stage. The last 30 seconds were mostly a blur, but that was amazing! By the time I reach the bottom of the stairs, I've already replayed what I can remember in my head. I vow to myself that next time I'll try to pay more attention to every detail, but I never want it to be any less thrilling.

Behind me I realize the announcer has been weighing Dale's fish. I manage to regain my awareness just in time to hear, "...new leader on the co-angler side! Boy oh boy, Boat 16 was on 'em today!"

When Dale joins me offstage, he's all smiles.

"That was awesome!" he tells me as he pats me solidly on the back.

"Awesome!" I confirm.

A couple young volunteers, a girl about 10 or 11 years old wearing an over-sized Triton Boats T-shirt, and a tall, skinny boy a couple years older than her, are waiting to quickly get the bass into the holding tanks on the release boat. "Nice fish," the boy compliments me as the girl fills the bag with green, treated water.

I smile and thank him graciously.

"Let's get that boat on the trailer and out of the way for everyone else," I suggest to Dale.

"Okay, I'll go get the truck," he offers.

As I make my way down to the boat, I encounter Carl headed to the scale with his bag.

"Did you get 'em today, Buckner?"

"Yeah, good day. Twenty-two, three."

He stops cold and looks me right in the eye for confirmation. "Twenty-two, three? Are you in the lead?"

"Yep. I didn't get a lot of bites, but I got the ones I was looking for," I tell him humbly. In my head I'm screaming about how happy I am, but I am very consciously trying to remain gracious in my victory. This is all so new to me.

"I'll say," he agrees. "Well, nice job, William. You were due."

"Thanks, it feels pretty..."

Suddenly the crowd noise swells. My attention is back on the voice coming over the speaker.

"Twenty-two pounds, FIVE ounces. Cam Severs pulls into the lead! Cam is no stranger to the leaderboard folks, but this is really something!"

Carl looks over his shoulder as he continues his trip to the scale. "Tough break, Buckner. I'm sure you'll still cash a pretty nice check though."

My feet start moving toward my boat, but my mind hasn't left the spot where I was standing. Some part of my brain knows that it might be best to keep moving. I put my hands on the bow of my boat and lift, pushing it back toward the water to loosen it from its beached position. I find my seat, turn the key, and ease the boat off of the shore. Now I'm floating in the middle of the chaos created by too many boats in too small of a space. Normally, this

194

scene makes me anxious and I try to find a spot out of the way on the outskirts. Right now, I'm just numb. Where is Dale, I wonder as I scan the line of trucks headed to the launch.

I shut off the motor and grab a seat on the front deck with the intent of stowing my rods. *Keep moving,* says my brain, but I've stopped listening. Fortunately, the rational part of my mind decides to contemplate what just happened. *Alright, so I didn't win. I stare at the small, white frog I used to catch my last fish. I didn't win. I thought I won, but I didn't win.* I draw a deep breath and exhale slowly. *I didn't win, but I did just weigh in my personal best tournament catch. Twenty-two, three would win 99 times out of 100 in a Wisconsin tournament. I did just prove to myself and everyone else that I have the skills to win, today just wasn't the right day. My confidence is very high that I will repeat this caliber of performance from this point forward. I am light years ahead of where I was last year. I remind myself, only I can control what happens to me. I can only hope to have the best possible day that I can have. If someone else's day results in a higher weight for them, that's beyond my control.*

I shift and raise the hand that I have been leaning on. The hot deck carpet has pressed a squiggly pattern of its fibers into my palm. I rub my hands together and look around at the boats hustling all around me. I'm really not competing against them, I think to myself. That's the amazing thing about this whole pursuit. My only real competition is the voice in my head. I know that if I continue down this path of mental conditioning and logical, scientific rationalization; if I fish at my own highest potential; if I am completely satisfied with my results, regardless of what place I finish; if I can breathe, focus, and fish; the first-place trophies will just become a by-product.

I recognize my truck and trailer backing down the ramp, so I hop into the driver's seat and fire up the big motor. I can't control the smile on my face. *Twenty-two, three?* I ask myself. This has been an amazing day!

* * *

"Well, that's the last one to weigh in," Dale tells me. "Looks like you got second. Congratulations. That's a good payday."

He offers his hand and I gladly shake it.

"Congratulations to you too, Dale. Third place on the co side! Nice job!"

The crowd begins to disperse a bit as many of the competitors who aren't going to cash a check decide to hit the road. It usually takes the tournament committee a couple minutes to analyze the results and prepare the checks and trophies for distribution.

Suddenly, a strong hand grabs me solidly around the back of my neck.

"So what did I miss. How'd it go today, Bro?" asks a playful, smiling Doug. "Doug! I didn't know you were gonna be here!" I return our manly embrace grabbing the back of his neck. "Glad to see your ugly mug, though! Thanks for coming."

Doug shoots back for the ugly comment. "So, you're hanging around like you think they're going to give you a check or something."

I laugh. "I think they are actually going to have a check for me today."

Doug's eyes get big and bright. "Seriously? That's awesome! What did you have?"

"Seriously," I confirm. "Twenty-two, three."

"Twenty-two, three?!" he responds with enough volume and enthusiasm that several people turn around to see what's going on. "Are you serious? You won?"

My excitement deflates just a little. "Actually, that will be second place today."

"Second? Oh, no. That's a kick in the jewels. Sheesh! What did it take to win?"

I lift my cap with one hand and run my other hand through my hair. "Cam had twenty-two, five," I inform him.

His eyes roll in disgust. "Ugh. Seavers? Well that figures."

Just as Doug says his name, I coincidentally spot Cam standing on the other side of the thin crowd. He's standing by himself. I wonder if his partner didn't catch enough to make a check? For a guy who just won a good-sized tournament, he doesn't look happy, confident, or satisfied. He looks tortured. I find myself feeling sorry for him. I consider going over to him and making amends, but quickly decide that would probably be a mistake.

"Yeah, it figures," I agree with Doug. "But you know what? Good for him," I tell him sincerely. "He had a great performance today, and he beat me. I don't hold that against him at all."

"Well you, sir, are a gentleman and a humanitarian," he tells me half-sarcastically.

"Thanks," I play along. "Oh, by the way, this is Dale, my partner from today." I take a step back from between the two of them. Dale smiles affably and extends his hand. Doug reciprocates.

"I'm Doug, William's brother-in-law. So did you put William on all those fish?" he asks and pokes me with his elbow.

Dale laughs politely then gets surprisingly serious. "No, I've never fished here before. We owe all of our fish to William. Honestly, it was pretty tough out there for most of the day. But, I've never fished with anyone as calm and focused as this guy. Anyone else would have had a meltdown, but not him." He pats me on the back. "This guy's a machine, a fishing cyborg!" he laughs. Knowing Doug like I do, I begin a countdown in my head until he punishes us all with a terrible Arnold Schwarzenegger impression. Three...two..

197

"I'll be bass," he drones in a deep, bad Austrian monotone.

Dale laughs sincerely. I laugh politely.

"Anyway, it was cool to see someone fish like that," Dale adds.

"Wow, that's really nice of you. Thanks," I tell him humbly.

"Man, I can't wait to fish a team tournament with the Bass Terminator," Doug tries to get a little more mileage out of the joke. He gets a little less laughter this time, but we do appreciate the effort.

The conversation reaches a moment of silence. We all look around, contemplating what we should talk about next.

"So how long does it take to put names on checks anyway?" Doug asks disgustedly.

"Yeah, it usually doesn't take too long. I'm sure they'll get started any minute," I respond.

"Hmm. Shouldn't be that hard," Doug grumbles, then perks up. "So how did you catch your fish anyway?"

Over the course of the next several minutes I recount the details of our day with Dale adding his own commentary and insight. It really does sound pretty epic, having taken a step back from it and hearing our story. Eventually, the tale reaches its end with a moment of silence. Again, we all looked around, trying to find the next topic of conversation.

At this point, it is clear from the faces of the crowd that this wait is getting ridiculous.

"Did they forget the checks back at the home office in Kentucky and have to send someone to pick them up?" Doug asks impatiently.

"This is getting a little...." I begin but am interrupted by a commotion from the other side of the crowd.

"You can't be serious!" a loud, angry voice accuses. I look in the general direction, but the crowd quickly surrounds the outburst, and I can't see what is going on.

"Unbelievable! Are you serious?" the voice continues angrier and louder. Instantly, I flash back to a time when that voice was directing those same comments at me. Cam! So what's that maniac yelling about now?

"I don't care what he told you! That is absolutely not true!" he protests. "Witnesses? Oh, bullshit! Have you lost your mind?"

Reflexively, we all move closer to see what's going on. Eventually, I spot Cam facing the tournament director, with two uniformed police officers and a DNR game warden standing behind him.

"So this is how you want to handle this?" Cam shouts at the tournament director. I couldn't hear the director's response, but Cam clearly didn't like it. "Right now? Are you crazy? This is crazy!" The two officers move up close behind him and each put a hand around his arms just above the elbow. They lean into him to get him moving. He resists for half a second, then thinks better of it. I guess even Cam isn't too crazy to realize that he would just be making things a lot worse.

"You're making a serious mistake!" he warns the director, as the officers lead him away from the crowd. "Unbelievable!" he shouts as they pull his arms behind him and apply the handcuffs. "Un-god-damned-believable!"

One of the officers reads him his rights as they walk toward the squad car. Then, just like on T.V., the other officer does that move where he guides the bad guy's head as he gets in the back seat. He slams the door shut and for the next several seconds everything is silent.

199

Suddenly the crowd erupts in a flurry of speculation, rumors and second-hand accounts.

"My cousin saw him."

"The DNR has been watching him for a long time."

"...lead weights in the fish's belly."

"I heard it's not the first time."

My mind is reeling as I try to put together what I just witnessed. The three of us haven't spoken a word. Doug turns to me slowly. His mouth is hanging open and his eyes are vacant. Suddenly, I see him regain his composure. He begins to smile and his face lights up. I have a feeling I can read his mind.

"I knew it!" he shouts. "I knew it and I told you!" He pokes me playfully in the chest with his finger. "I told you he was greasy! Ha! I told you!"

I smile at his excitement. "All right, Sherlock. That will do."

He raises his eyebrows and stares at me. "Well?" He waits, then wags his eyebrows at me. "Well?"

Finally, I tell him what he wants in an effort to shut him up. Truth is, I know it probably will not work.

I clear my throat. "You were right, Doug."

"I know," he celebrates, "because I'm always right!"

Now I raise my eyebrows at him. He pauses for a second, then realizes what I'm getting at.

He clears his throat. "Alright. Apparently, there may be something to your new approach to fishing." He extends his hand and we shake. "Congratulations, brother. Really amazing performance."

"Congratulations is right," Dale interjects and grabs my hand for his turn to shake it. "I believe you just won this tournament."

"Oh, my God," I utter in astonishment. It hadn't dawned on me yet. This is my personal best tournament finish by a long shot. "Do you really think I won?"

Doug smiles at me. "I don't think the winner typically gets a ride home from the tournament in a police car."

"I suppose not," I agree.

"It looks to me like you had the best weight today. If my understanding of tournament fishing is correct,...that makes you the winner."

The smile spreads slowly across my face as this thought sinks in. *I knew it. I knew it!* says the voice in my head. I should have trusted my gut. When I caught that last fish, I felt like I had won. I was absolutely in tune with my environment at that point, and I was certain I had just won. This is all so new to me, but I need to remember this lesson and trust my gut.

Suddenly it dawns on me that I need to call Trixie. I can't tell you how long I've been looking forward to the day I could make this call.

I dig into my pocket searching for my iPhone when the P.A. systems crackles to life with the tournament director's voice.

"I'm terribly sorry about that little distraction, folks." The crowd responds with nervous laughter, followed by more buzzing of rumors. He continues, "It's been an interesting afternoon to say the least. In any case, I believe we have this all figured out now." He waits for a smattering of applause. "Let's give away some money and trophies!" More applause.

"Ladies and gentlemen, with a limit of fish weighing 22 pounds and 3 ounces...taking home $7,499... your champion today...from Chippewa Falls, Wisconsin..." He points me out in the crowd. "Mr. William Buckner!"

There is a decent amount of applause, and several pats on the back, as I make my way through the crowd toward the stage. I really am trying to notice and remember as many details as possible about how this feels and looks and sounds. This scene will power my future visualization exercises. I remember the fishing cyborg comment Dale made and laugh to myself.

As I climb the stairs to the stage, the director offers a congratulatory handshake, then passes me the first-place trophy. It's a fairly simple, but important-looking, wooden plaque with a gold-inlayed leaping bass. It is surprisingly heavier than it looks. I smile and hold it up for the crowd to see.

"So, tell us a little about your day," the director instructs. He holds the mic in front of my face rather than letting me hold it myself. Before I can answer, he pulls the mic back to himself and asks, "Did you think you'd catch that kind of a bag today? Were you on 'em in practice?"

I look out at the crowd and realize that I am quite unaccustomed to having this many people listening to what I have to say about fishing. For a half a second I am rattled, but I take a deep breath and decide to enjoy the spotlight.

"I did have a good practice. I was pretty sure it would be a good day."

He nods his approval at my answer. "So tell us how you caught 'em."

I realize that the information he's looking for is mostly inconsequential, but it's the standard post-tournament interview. "The first four hit a Texas-rigged creature bait," I oblige. And the last fish hit a frog."

He nods more enthusiastically and tips the microphone back to him. "Brand and color?"

202

"Um... well, it was a Sweet Beaver by Reaction Innovations, I guess it was green pumpkin with a little chartreuse..."

"So, like a Spanish Fly or Corn Dog color, or maybe Dirty Sanchez?"
"Honestly, I'm not sure."

"What size weight?"

"Half ounce," I respond courteously, but I decide that I want to steer this conversation a bit. Before he can ask a follow up I add, "I think the real key today was being patient and staying focused. Honestly, it was tough out there for me most of the day. I only had five bites today. But I think by staying calm when it was not going well, I was able to perform when the bites did finally come."

He looks surprised and a little impressed. "Interesting." He pauses, then finds his place back in his rehearsed interview questions.

"Did you lock through today?"

"No. We ran quite a ways south, but we stayed in this pool."

"Mmm hmm. Anything else you'd like to add?"

I take a second to consider my options.

"I guess it was my day, today."

He seems content with our exchange. "Let's hear it again for William Buckner!"

* * *

"Hello?" her sweet voice answers.

"Hey, Trix! How are you, dear?"

"Good, William. We were just drawing on Dacey's marker board and wondering when you would be home."

"I just got on the road, so I'll be there in about two hours."

"Oh, good. We've missed you."

I chuckle. "I've missed you too, dear."

There's a brief pause then she asks in a chipper voice, "So, did you win?" She always asks just like that. Even after all these years, she still asks as if it's entirely possible, even likely, that I did win. I'm lucky to have her.

"Trix, it's been a crazy day. Man, have I got a story for you."

She doesn't respond right away. "So, did you win?"

"Trix..."

"You won, didn't you?" The excitement is building in her voice. "William, did you win?"

"I won, Trixie." My voice cracks a bit as I say it.

There is a second of silence on the line... then an enthusiastic scream. Then silence...then another scream. Then I hear what sounds like Dacey crying.

"No sweetie, don't cry," I hear Trixie consoling her. "It's okay. I'm sorry. I was just excited."

"It's okay, Dacey," I speak into the phone even though I realize she probably can't hear me.

Trixie returns to the phone. "I scared Dacey," she says sheepishly. Then off the phone she says, "Yes, Daddy is fine. He's on his way home. He just won his big tournament." Then back into the phone, "Dacey says congratulations and she is very proud of you."

I sniff back a tear, then try to mask it by clearing my throat. "Tell her thanks."

"I will," she promises enthusiastically. "Oh, honey that's such great news! You won!" she reminds me as if I'd forgotten. "Please hurry home, but drive safely."

"I will, dear."

"I can't wait to hear every detail. I'll have your favorite meal ready when you get here," she promises.

"You're the best, Trixie," I tell her sincerely.

"No, you're the best," she responds, "and now you have a trophy to prove it."

Ch 30
Peace

"Hey, buddy," I greet Doug as he climbs into the passenger seat and slams the door.

"Hey, William." He begins to take a sip of coffee from the thermos cup he brought with him when he stops suddenly and looks at me with mock disgust. "You wore your fancy, sponsor, pimp shirt? You think a tournament might break out?"

"Miss Charlotte asked me to wear it," I defend myself. "She thinks the kids will think it's cool."

"Oh, you're cool all right," he teases.

I shake my head and laugh. "I think this is going to be fun today."

His tone changes from fake annoyed to friendly. "I totally agree. Thanks for getting me involved."

"My pleasure. I had a feeling you'd like it." For a guy who doesn't have any kids of his own, he really does seem to enjoy them. *Maybe it's because he's so childish,* I laugh to myself.

Then his eyes open wide like he just remembered something important. "Did you hear any of the details about Cam?"

"Details? No, not really...I mean, I heard he was officially disqualified for cheating. Have you heard more than that?"

"Yeah. A guy at my work is cousins with that DNR officer who was at the tournament when they dragged him away."

"Really?...So, what happened?" I demand impatiently.

"Well, I guess he had a big basket of fish, actually two baskets of nice fish, stashed way up in the back of a pad flat in some little, secluded backwater area."

"The 'Bat Cave'," I say aloud. I meant to just think it but the words spilled out of my mouth. Doug must not have heard me, or maybe didn't understand.

He continued.

"Apparently, a local had seen him placing these big metal baskets out there during the week. The local guy thought that was suspicious enough that he came back out there that evening and found them filled with big bass. He called the DNR and they went out there and marked all the fish and waited to see what would happen."

"No way! A sting operation?" I gasp.

"So, I guess Cam kept working on his co-angler all day and eventually convinced the guy that it was a good idea. He had nice limits for both of them. This guy was definitely going to win a nice check for himself, plus Cam gave him $500 in cash."

"No way!"

"But after they weighed them in, the co-angler, Mark...Mark Soronski?...or maybe Soleski?...Something-ski...I can't remember...from Illinois, I think. So, this Mark guy from Illinois went to the tournament director behind Cam's back and confessed to the whole thing."

"No way!"

"Yes way! So, Mark is banned from fishing in any more tournaments, but they didn't press charges against him. Cam, on the other hand, might be in pretty serious trouble. They're actually conducting a full investigation to try to determine if this is an isolated incident, or if he's been 'winning' tournaments like this for years."

"Yikes!" I respond, as if I can feel his pain.

"Yikes nothing. The tournament is the easy part. Don't forget arson and insurance fraud," Doug reminds me.

Then he gives me a goofy look and in his best crotchety old man voice says, "And I would have got away with it, if it hadn't been for those meddling kids!" He finishes his story with a Scooby-Doo "Hee-hee-hee-hee."

I give him half a laugh and roll my eyes while pulling the truck into a space and putting it in park. Doug waits for my response. I think about the details of the story for a couple seconds. Finally, I turn to him.

"Is it weird that I sort of feel sorry for him?"

"Yes, it's weird!" he answers quickly. "That guy is a cheating scumbag! How would he be worthy of your pity?"

"I guess I was just thinking how terrible it would feel to live like that. I mean, he doesn't need the money. Is it ego? Has he been going through all that trouble just to make sure he upholds his reputation as a good fisherman? Can you imagine the pressure you'd feel from that much lying?"

Doug looks at me like I'm crazy. "No, I can't imagine what it would feel like to be a liar and a cheater."

"No, of course not. I just mean... I'm not suggesting that there's any justification for what he's done. I think it sucks and I think he should pay for it. I'm not sure why, but I'm just not feeling all that angry at him. Maybe I've just put him so far behind me at this point that he's not worth wasting any of my time or energy worrying about. I would hate for any negative thoughts about him to taint my fishing."

Doug laughs. "You really are a fishing cyborg."

I smile, "Let's go teach some kids the right way to fish."

As we walk across the parking lot, I realize that I'm a little bit nervous. But it's not a scared kind of nervous, it's more of an excited nervous. I have an overwhelming feeling that I'm finally on track to live my life's purpose. Sharing what I know about fishing, in the hope that I might inspire or guide or direct someone else to experience the passion and joy I feel about this activity, is simply the right thing to do. I take a deep, centering breath. My thoughts are clear, my confidence is high and my heart is open.

I lean on the silver bar and push the door that had been locked when Dacey and I first visited a couple months earlier. Doug and I step into the hallway. Ahead of us we can hear the sound of happy children playing.

"I wonder if that's our group?" Doug asks. I'm pretty sure I can hear the same nervous excitement I'm feeling in his voice.

Suddenly, the nice lady from my last visit emerges from a doorway down the hall on the right. She is surprised and delighted to find us headed her way.

"Oh, Mr. Buckner, it's so nice to see you! And this must be your brother!" She approaches quickly with a hand extended toward Doug. "It's so nice to meet you! I'm Charlotte Lautner. Everyone here calls me Miss Charlotte."

Doug smiles warmly and shakes her hand. "Very nice to meet you, Miss Charlotte. I'm Doug."

"I'm so pleased you've decided to join us. This is so generous of both of you and I can promise you the children appreciate it."

210

"It's our pleasure," I assure her.

"Did we get a good turnout?" Doug asks, sounding a bit childlike himself.

"Oh, excellent," she reports. "There are 18 children from six to 12 years old. Five of them are girls!" Miss Charlotte's smile is infectious.

"That's great!" I tell her. "When can we get started?"

"If you're ready, we can start now," she smiles and motions us to follow her. We leave the relatively dim light of the hallway and enter a bright classroom setting. There are several groups of children spread throughout the room, laughing and talking.

They settle themselves and quiet down quickly when they notice us with Miss Charlotte.

"Excellent news," she announces. "We are very lucky to have two very accomplished instructors for our fishing program this year. They have taken time off from their busy tournament fishing schedules to share their knowledge with us."

Doug makes eye contact with me and smiles sheepishly. I give him a small shrug and a nod, indicating to just go with it. Of course it's a slight exaggeration, but I can't see any benefit from correcting her in front of the kids.

"Children, please help me in welcoming Mr. Doug Pratt and Mr. Bill Buckner." The children applaud politely.

Out of the corner of my eye, I catch Doug wincing as if someone just made him smell an old sweat sock. I know his pain is partly sympathetic for me and partly him waiting for my reaction to being called Bill instead of William. But for the first time I can remember, I don't feel bad at all about being Bill Buckner. Miss Charlotte didn't intend anything but respect when she introduced me. It's my name. So what if it happens to be the same name as a professional baseball player? Doesn't that actually make it kind of a cool name to have? The fact is, Bill Buckner, the ball player, had a long, above-average, successful career. So what if he dropped that one ball? The reason he was even playing in the World Series is because he had made that same play successfully thousands of times. How many players never make it to the World Series? How many never make it to the Major Leagues? How could I possibly be embarrassed to be associated with him?

I shoot Doug a subtle nod and a smile to let him know everything is all right. Then I face my students.

"Good morning, everyone," I say clearly and confidently. "Like Miss Charlotte said, my name is Bill. Now, who wants to learn how to catch some fish?"

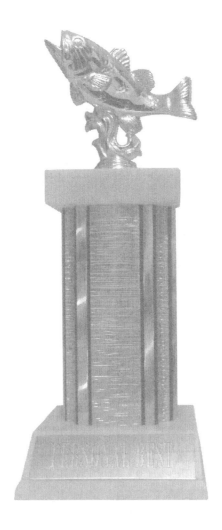

www.personalbestfishingandlife.com

Made in the USA
Lexington, KY
20 February 2017